AF086066

PINQUO

Colin Thiele (pronounced Tee-lee) has published almost a hundred books during a writing career that spans more than fifty years.

He was born in Eudunda, South Australia, and spent his child hood on a farm in the nearby ranges. He was schooled in the area, then went to the University of Adelaide where he was an outstandingly successful student.

After service in the RAAF during the Second World War he became a high school teacher and college lecturer, and eventually a principal and director. In 1945 he married Rhonda Gill, a teacher and artist, and they had two daughters – Janne and Sandy.

It was in 1958, during a sea voyage to the United States to take up a Fulbright Scholarship, that Colin Thiele wrote the first of his children's books. Since then he has become one of the best known and loved of Australian authors, and has received many awards and commendations for his work. In 1977 he was awarded the high honour of Companion of the Order of Australia (AC) for services to literature and education.

Feature films and television programs based on his books (*Storm Boy, Blue Fin, The Fire in the Stone, The Water Trolley*, and *Sun on the Stubble*) have been seen and acclaimed in many countries, and his work has been published extensively overseas – in China, Japan, Russia, South Africa and North America, England, and ten European countries.

In 1993 Colin and Rhonda Thiele moved to Dayboro, a small town north of Brisbane. Colin passed away in 2006.

Other Children's Books by Colin Thiele:

Sun on the Stubble
Sun on the Stubble Picture Book
Storm Boy
Storm Boy and other Stories
Blue Fin
February Dragon
The Undercover Secret
The Fire in the Stone
Albatross Two (Fight Against Albatross Two)
Magpie Island
River Murray Mary
The Hammerhead Light
The Sknuks
Songs for my Thongs
Coorong Captive
Flip-Flop and Tiger Snake
Gloop the Bunyip
Mrs Munch and Puffing Billy
Klontarf
Stories Short & Tall

COLIN THIELE

PINQUO

Published by New Holland Publishers
Sydney

Level 1, 178 Fox Valley Road, Wahroonga, NSW 2076, Australia

newhollandpublishers.com

First Published by Rigby Publishers 1983
Paperback edition 1986
Reprinted by Weldon Publishing 1992
Reprinted by Lansdowne Publishing Pty Ltd 1996
Reprinted by New Holland Publishers 2005
Reprinted 2007, 2010, 2015, 2021, 2023

Copyright © 2010 New Holland Publishers
Copyright © 1983 Colin Thiele
Copyright © 2005 design: Lansdowne Publishing Pty Ltd

Wholly designed in Australia
Typeset by Caxtons Pty Ltd, Adelaide

Thiele, Colin, 1920–2006
    Pinquo.
    For children.
    ISBN 9781741102383
    1. Penguins – Juvenile fiction. I. Title

All rights reserved. No part of this publication may be reproduced, stored
in a retrieval system or transmitted, in any form or by any means, electronic,
mechanical, photocopying, recording or otherwise, without the prior written
permission of the publishers and copyright holders.

Text Illustrations by Mary Milton
Cover design: Donnah Luttrell
Cover photograph from i-stock images
Printed in Australia by Pegasus Print Group

Keep up with New Holland Publishers:
 NewHollandPublishers
 @newhollandpublishers

Adopt a Penguin at www.penguinfoundation.org.au

TO LITTLE PINQUO

Who saved our lives and lost his own.

Erected by the grateful people of Sickle Bay.

We will never forget him.

Prologue

There is a monument in the little town of Sickle Bay. It stands in the middle of an open space near the jetty. Around it there is a small patch of green lawn and a garden border that is always kept neat and tidy.

The monument is very simple. It is just a narrow column of stone about as high as a man. And at the top is a life-sized statue of a small creature standing with its flippers held out and its head turned slightly as if its sharp eyes are gazing out across the bay to the great ocean that sweeps far away towards Antarctica from the curving coast of Australia.

A bronze plaque has been fixed to the stone column.

The monument is really the ending of a strange and wonderful story. As the plaque says, it is something that the people of Sickle Bay will never forget. It will be handed down by mothers and fathers to their children, and to their children's children, for hundreds of years.

This is the story.

1

Pinquo was a penguin. His home was a rocky burrow near the entrance to Sickle Bay. Hundreds of his friends lived there too, in hollows along the coast or in holes dug into the sedge-covered sandhills near by. He weighed exactly one kilogram and when he stood up he was thirty-three centimetres high. That meant that he was the smallest kind of penguin in the world. Scientists called him the Little Blue, but ordinary people said he was a Fairy Penguin. That was a beautiful and proper name for someone like Pinquo.

Pinquo was a sort of poem. His eyes were like little circles of moonlight and his feathers were soft and strong. On his back they were the colour of blue steel but his chest was as clean and white as laundered linen. At daybreak each morning he went down to the sea to fish. He swam and skipped and dived faster than the blink of an eye. He darted and swung and looped this way and that like a bird swooping about in the high clear sky. But Pinquo was flying under the water.

Pinquo was a clown. At dusk each evening he waddled up the beach towards his burrow like a small plump gentleman. He stood preening himself very particularly for a while; then he moved his flippers up and down slowly and started to sing — a dreadful song that sounded like a donkey in pain. At sea he clowned with his friends too, flipping water about or porpoising along like a skipping rocket — under the surface, up into the air, and back under again, for the sheer joy and speed of it.

Pinquo was a lovely, gentle, wonderful creature.

2

It was Kirsty who first gave Pinquo his name. One Saturday morning in October, when she and her brother, Tim, were exploring the rock pools by the shore, she heard a strange sound.

'Listen,' she said. 'What's that?'

Tim stopped fossicking for shells and cocked his head. 'Someone's calling out,' he said. 'He must be hurt.' Kirsty scoffed, 'It's not a person.'

'What, then?'

'An animal or a bird.'

The noise was a mixture of sounds — a cry, a squeak, a slap, a bark.

'It's coming from the rocks,' Tim said. He pointed to the low cliffs and ledges along the shore, 'Up there.'

They both scrambled up, pausing every now and then to pinpoint the spot where the sound was coming from. And so they found Pinquo. He was lying in a cleft near the entrance to his burrow. A rock had been dislodged somehow and it had fallen down and pinned one of his flippers.

'It's a penguin,' said Tim, 'a little Fairy.'

Kirsty knelt down and looked closely. 'He's

frightened and he's hurt,' she said. 'Look, there's blood on his flipper.'

'It could be broken,' said Tim. 'We'll have to free him. He'll die if we don't.'

She took off her jacket and used the sleeves like a pair of gloves. Then she reached over with both hands to seize him by the body. 'I'll hold him and you see if you can shift the rock.'

At first Pinquo was angry and alarmed. He pecked and struggled and flapped with his other flipper, but when Tim heaved the stone away and Kirsty lifted him up gently and held him against her chest he seemed to realise that they were trying to help him.

'What now?' Tim asked.

'I don't think we should let him go.'

'Why not?'

'I think his flipper is crushed. If he can't swim or catch fish he'll starve.'

'He's got a ruff round his neck. What does that mean?'

'Perhaps it shows whether he's a boy or a girl.'

Tim looked about uneasily. The sun was climbing and the day was moving towards noon. 'What are you going to do, then? You can't hold him here all day.'

Kirsty stood up suddenly. 'I know,' she said. 'We'll take him to Dr Piper.'

Dr Piper was not a doctor of medicine. He was a scientist. Once he had been the director of a big museum but he had retired long ago and come to live in Sickle Bay. He was an expert on sea plants and sea shells but he knew a lot about birds and animals too, and he loved to mooch about on the seashore almost as much as Kirsty did. He had red cheeks and bright eyes and a big shock of white hair.

'Hullo, Kirsty Kemp,' he said as soon as he had opened the door. 'What on earth have you got there?'

'It's a little Fairy,' Kirsty answered. 'And he's been hurt.'

'A rock fell on him,' Tim added. 'On his flipper.'

Dr Piper clicked his tongue sadly. 'Tch, tch, tch. Let me have a look.'

He reached out and took Pinquo. He had a special way of doing it, so that the little penguin didn't seem to struggle at all.

'He's only a baby,' Dr Piper said. 'He's only seven weeks old.'

'Is that all?' answered Kirsty. 'How can you tell?'

'By the ruff round his neck.'

Tim came closer. 'We wondered what that meant.'

'He'll lose it within a week or two. He's already lost all his baby down and put on his blue coat. He's nearly ready to go to sea.'

'Could he manage?'

Dr Piper handled the blood-stained flipper carefully. 'Not with this. He couldn't swim properly. A shark or a leopard seal would be sure to get him.'

Kirsty was sad. 'How horrible.'

Tim was always practical. 'What's going to happen to him?'

Dr Piper walked off through the kitchen towards the back door. 'I guess I'd better keep him here for a few weeks. I think he's old enough to eat without help from his parents.'

They followed him out into the backyard where there were all kinds of boxes and cages and wire-netting yards. He put Pinquo into one of the big cages with a box in one corner like a dark, solid burrow.

'Can we come each day and help you look after him?' Kirsty asked. Dr Piper smiled such a big smile that it filled his face. 'Of course,' he said. 'I expect you to.'

At the front door Kirsty suddenly turned. 'What are we going to call him? He has to have a name.'

'He already has a name,' answered Dr Piper, laughing. 'It's *Eudyptula minor*.'

'That's hopeless,' said Tim.

Kirsty wrinkled her nose in disgust. 'I mean a special name — just for him.' They could see that Dr Piper was still chuckling.

'What about "Bluey"?' he suggested. 'His blue feathers will soon be very beautiful.'

'That's too common,' Kirsty answered. 'And anyway, his chest is shining white, like new paint.'

Dr Piper looked serious but his eyes still danced with merriment. 'What about "Pinto",' he said. 'That comes from a Spanish word — *pintado*. It means "painted".'

Kirsty tasted the name on her tongue. 'I like that,' she answered, 'but it sounds more like a horse than a bird. It should have a *g* or a *q* in it for a penguin.'

'So it should,' agreed Dr Piper.

Kirsty looked doubtful. 'Pingo? No, I don't like that.'

'Neither do I,' said Tim. 'It sounds like ping-pong.'

Then Kirsty's eyes lit up. 'Pinquo,' she said out loud. 'That's it. Pinquo.'

'Yes,' said Tim.

'Yes, that's good,' said Dr Piper. 'Pinquo the penguin.'

And so it was agreed. From that moment Pinquo was Pinquo.

3

Kirsty and Tim ran home to tell their mother. They went past Dr Piper's white picket fence, past Mrs Hempel's old house next door, past the open space near the head of the jetty, and turned into the main street. There was really only one street in the town so it had to be the main one anyway. Sickle Bay was such a tiny place that there were only twenty or thirty houses and a hundred people there altogether.

They ran up past the Commercial Hotel, and Mr Harper's bakery, past the little post office where Mrs Martin, the postmistress, was standing in the doorway looking as faded as an old stamp, past the café and the newsagent and the grocery shop, until they finally tumbled in at their own gate.

'Mum,' Kirsty called, bursting in through the front door. 'Mum, what do you think?'

There was no one at home.

'She must be helping Dad,' Tim said. 'Come and see.'

They plunged out again and ran next door where their father had his workshop and petrol station. Their mother was standing beside the pump, filling the tank of somebody's car.

'Mum, guess what! We've found a penguin.' Kirsty stood panting, brimming with excitement.

'Its wing is broken,' Tim added.

Their mother got such a surprise that she accidentally overfilled the tank and spilt petrol all over the place.

'Oh, blast,' she said angrily.

'But he's going to be all right,' Kirsty said eagerly. 'Well, we think he is.'

Mrs Kemp screwed the cap back on the tank, wiped up some of the mess, and took the money from the driver. Then she turned to Kirsty and Tim. 'Now look, you two,' she said. 'We are not having a pet penguin. Absolutely not. I'm fed up — cats, dogs, rabbits, frogs, tadpoles, possums, silkworms, and sick seabirds. All kinds of cripples and waifs and strays. The backyard is like a zoo. It's starting to stink.'

Kirsty tried to put her mother straight. 'But Mum . . .'

'No, Kirsty.'

Tim joined in.

'Mum, we're just trying to tell you . . .'

'No'.

At that moment their father walked out of the workshop with grease all over his clothes and a big spanner in his hand. He looked at them, partly angry and partly amused.

'You heard what your mother said: no pet penguins.'

'But Dad . . .'

'No pet penguins.'

'Dad we're only trying to . . .'

'To help a poor helpless seabird. I know, I know. I've heard it all before.'

Kirsty was bursting with frustration. She had tears in her eyes. 'Will you just listen to us?' she blurted out loudly. 'The penguin is at Dr Piper's place.'

Her father and mother were suddenly silent.

'Oh,' said her father after a while.

'I see,' said her mother.

'Well . . .,' said her father.

'That's different,' said her mother.

Kirsty turned away and wiped her eyes quickly with the back of her hand. 'If only you'd listened,' she said sulkily, 'instead of . . .'

Her father put his arm round her shoulders. 'Instead of jumping to conclusions? But you really are a bit of a Florence Nightingale, aren't you?'

Kirsty smiled wanly. 'But they'd die if we didn't help them. The penguin would have died.'

'We have to see Dr Piper again,' Tim said. 'We're going back tomorrow.'

'To help with the penguin?'

'Yes. He's called Pinquo.'

Their father raised his eyebrows.

'Pinquo. That's an interesting name.'

'Yes. Kirsty thought of it.'

Their mother shook her head. 'For heaven's sake,' she said. She looked at her watch. 'Well I guess I'd better go in and get some lunch for all of us — especially for a couple of young penguins with appetites like whales.' She walked a few steps and paused again.

'And remember. As long as this Pinko-Ninko is with Dr Piper, that's fine. But that's where he stays.'

'Pinquo,' said Kirsty.

'What's that?'

'Pinquo, not Ninko.'

'Ninko, nincompoop, whatever his name is, he stays with Dr Piper. Right?'

'Yes, Mum.'

'He does *not* come here. Never.'

'No, Mum.'

'Good. Let's go in and have some lunch.'

4

Mr and Mrs Kemp liked to sleep in on Sunday mornings. Usually Kirsty and Tim stayed in bed too, because they knew that if they did get up they would have to tiptoe very quietly about the house or play a game of Scrabble in the kitchen. But this morning they both got up early and made their own breakfast because they were eager to visit Dr Piper and Pinquo.

It was a beautiful October morning. The water in the bay was a sheet of glass and the sand on the long curving beach glowed like yellow gold. The curve of sand and water had given Sickle Bay its name. There was even a rocky platform at the end of it that looked like a handle, and the wet sand at the edge of the water shone in the sun as sharply as a polished blade. As Kirsty and Tim walked past the jetty a fishing boat cast off and putt-putted across the bay towards the open sea, breaking up the mirror with an arrowhead of ripples.

From time to time Tim had to trot to keep up with Kirsty. She was ten and he was only nine, and when she was in a hurry she strode out with her long legs like a thoroughbred. He was hoping she would get the pony she had been promised for her eleventh birthday because then she could go galloping off across the paddocks and he would be left to go about his own business on his bike.

Although it was barely eight o'clock when they reached Dr Piper's place he was already waiting for them. 'Come in, come in,' he said heartily. 'You want to see the patient?'

'Yes, please,' said Kirsty. 'How is he?'

'Fine, fine.' Dr Piper led the way out to the backyard. 'But we have a job to do, and I need your help.'

Kirsty was curious. 'Oh?'

'Yes. We have to put a splint on his flipper.'

'Is it broken, then?' asked Tim.

'I think so. It's hard to be certain without an X-ray. But I'm sure the bone has been damaged.'

Pinquo was hiding in his box-burrow when they reached his cage and so Dr Piper put his hands inside very carefully and drew him out.

'Has he eaten anything yet?' asked Kirsty.

'Yes, last night. I got some fish for him. But I had to pretend I was mum and dad. You should have seen me. It was a circus and I was the clown.' Dr Piper laughed, and so did Kirsty and Tim.

'Now then,' he went on, 'I want you to hold him, Kirsty, while Tim and I put on the splint.' He took some bandages and two flat pieces of plywood that he had cut to the right size and shape. Then, very gently, he placed the damaged part of Pinquo's flipper between them and asked Tim to hold the wood firmly while he bound it in position with adhesive tape. He did it beautifully, like a doctor. When it was finished poor Pinquo looked as if he had a big wooden sandwich on his arm.

'He won't be able to bend his wing,' Tim said.

'He can't bend it in any case,' answered Dr Piper. 'A flipper is not like a wing. There are no joints.' Tim was surprised, 'I didn't know that.'

'Penguins may have had wings long ago,' Dr Piper went on, 'but they've gradually changed for use in the sea. The bones are broader and flatter to take the thrust of the water, and the joints are fused. The flipper is really a kind of paddle.'

'Can't he even fold it?' asked Kirsty.

'No, he never does. It always sticks out from his body like an arm. That's why people like to make jokes about it and shake hands with it. Penguins look like little people.'

Kirsty put Pinquo down gently. 'They're beautiful little people,' she said.

They stood watching for a minute or two to see whether Pinquo would be upset by the splints.

'Do you think he needs a drink — some fresh water?' Kirsty asked after a while.

'It wouldn't hurt,' answered Dr Piper. 'But of course there's no fresh water in the sea.'

For the second time that morning Tim looked up in astonishment. 'Does he drink sea water, then?'

'He can — if he wants to.'

'You'd think he'd die.'

'Not at all. He can get rid of the extra salt in

his body through special passages in his nose; it just drops off the end of his bill.'

Tim was speechless. 'That's wonderful,' he said at last.

Dr Piper smiled hugely like a big cherub. 'Of course it's wonderful. The whole world is wonderful. Everything is made to fit into its place. And you and Kirsty are the most wonderful of all. Just look at the way you are made.'

Tim grinned wryly. 'Sometimes Mum and Dad don't think we're very wonderful.'

Dr Piper laughed out loud. Then he looked at them both with that quizzical glance of his. 'They do really — deep down.'

Kirsty pulled a face. 'Not when we bring home a penguin, they don't.'

'Didn't they like the idea?'

'Mum almost had a fit. She thought we were going to keep Pinquo at our place.'

'I'm sure they'd change their minds if they got to know him properly.'

Dr Piper packed up his tools and went back into the kitchen. 'Just wait there for a minute,' he said. 'We'll try to give him a bit more to eat.' A moment later he returned with a bowl of small fish. He look at Pinquo sternly. 'You've got a huge appetite, my boy,' he said. 'You're going to cost me a fortune in food.'

'Can you get enough?' Kirsty asked anxiously.

'I've spoken to Charlie Bates. He says he can supply as much as I need.'

'Oh, yes,' Tim said. 'We saw him going out on

his boat this morning.'

Dr Piper got down on his hands and knees in Pinquo's cage with the bowl of fish pieces beside him.

'Why in the world do you have to do that?' asked Tim.

'I have to be mum and dad. You haven't seen the half of it yet.'

He knelt beside Pinquo's burrow and made a strange noise, trying to imitate a penguin. Then he took some bits of fish in his hand and shaped his fingers like an open beak. Slowly he arched his arm above Pinquo's head and brought the pointed hand down towards it. Kirsty and Tim watched in astonishment. Suddenly Pinquo opened his bill and thrust it upwards, and Dr Piper popped the fish far back into his throat so that he could gulp it down. Then he seized some more fish from the bowl and repeated the performance.

'That's marvellous,' said Kirsty softly. 'He's eating like a champion.'

'He's eating like a greedy gob,' answered Dr Piper. 'No manners at all.' He scooped up another handful and let Pinquo gobble it down. 'But we're really very lucky,' he said after a while. 'Three or four weeks ago he would probably have been too small to feed like this. He would have died of starvation.'

'Why do you have to feed him like that?' Tim asked. 'It looks crazy.'

Dr Piper chuckled. 'Of course it does. But that's how his mum and dad feed him — by regurgitating food they've caught in the sea.'

He stood up slowly. 'Your turn tonight, Kirsty,' he said with a grin, and yours tomorrow, Tim.' He sniffed at himself and pulled a wry face. 'I smell like a fish,' he said. 'I don't think I'll ever be normal again.'

They went back into the house at last, and Dr Piper washed and scrubbed his hands in hot water. He stood in the doorway of the bathroom, drying his hands on a big towel.

'I think we've earned ourselves some morning tea and a biscuit, don't you?'

'Yes, please.'

Kirsty watched while he filled the kettle. 'How long will Pinquo have to wear his splints?' she asked.

'Six or seven weeks I should say. Perhaps even longer.'

'Gosh, it'll be December by then. Almost Christmas time.'

'Yes, it will.'

'Won't that be too late for him to go back to the sea with all the others?'

'I don't think so.'

She looked at him anxiously. 'Will he really be all right?'

He smiled broadly. 'I'm sure he will. I think we're going to see much more of Pinquo before we're finished.'

Dr Piper was right.

5

For the next six weeks Kirsty and Tim visited Dr Piper every day — sometimes the one, sometimes the other, and sometimes both of them together. During the week it was usually a quick dash before or after school, but on Saturdays and Sundays they could dawdle as long as they liked and have a cup of tea or a drink of fruit juice with Dr Piper.

Pinquo grew quickly. Before long he had lost the ruff around his neck just as Dr Piper had said he would, and was walking about importantly. He still carried the splint with him, of course, holding out his flipper like someone with a double bat about to play a game of ping-pong. Dr Piper let him have the run of the whole backyard with lots of boxes and cubbies where he could poke and scratch about and pretend he had the best penguin burrow in the world.

Within a week or two he was so tame that Kirsty and Tim could touch him whenever they liked, and by the middle of November he was following Dr Piper everywhere like a little blue dwarf.

'You're almost ready to look after yourself,'

Dr Piper said one day. 'Another week and I think we'll take off those splints. Then we'll soon see if you can cope or not.'

And so, on the following Saturday morning, Kirsty and Tim hurried round to help with Pinquo's 'operation'. It was quite a ceremony. Although he was so tame by now that he walked up to them like an old friend, he was not quite so happy when Dr Piper started to peel off the tape that held the splints together.

'Don't be a sook,' he said. 'You're a big grown-up fellow.'

Pinquo cocked his head as if to say, 'Don't give me soft soap.'

Luckily it took no more than a few minutes to strip off the splints. It was quite painless. Dr Piper ran his fingers up and down the flipper, feeling the bone gently for signs of damage.

'It feels good,' he said after a while. 'I think it's knitted well. It should be as strong as ever.' He paused again, looking critically at the flipper. 'Unfortunately he's always going to have a bit of a kink in it where the rock first struck.' He leant forward and pointed. 'Just there . . . see.'

'Yes,' said Tim. 'There's a dip in the edge.'

Kirsty eyed Pinquo carefully. 'I think he's a bit lopsided too,' she said at last. 'His left flipper droops a bit more than his right.'

Dr Piper considered the point. 'It could just be the effect of the splints. In that case it will right itself as his muscles get stronger. But he could have suffered permanent damage to his shoulder. If that's so I'm afraid he'll have a droop for the rest of his life.'

Kirsty leaned forward and tickled Pinquo under the chin. It was something he seemed to like very much. 'Never mind,' she said, 'we'll look after you, Pinquo. We really will.'

Dr Piper scratched his nose slowly. 'I'm not so sure we'll be able to,' he said. 'Once Pinquo goes to sea we may not see him again for years.'

Kirsty sat up with a start. 'Not see him again?' she cried. 'What do you mean?'

'He'll swim far away from here — perhaps a thousand kilometres or more.'

Tim was flabbergasted. 'A *thousand* kilometres.'

'Yes. Some do it very quickly — within a month or two. They've been tagged, or banded, and then found again.'

'What do they do all that time?'

'They just swim about, and fish, and grow strong I guess. And then at last they come back here to breed.'

Kirsty was glum.

'After a year?' she asked in a small voice.

'More likely two or three years. Maybe even longer.'

She looked at Pinquo sadly. 'We'll be strangers by then. He'll have forgotten all about us.'

'We could band him,' Dr Piper suggested, 'although with that gammy flipper of his we'd probably recognise him anywhere. They always come back to their old burrow, or one close by.'

'When . . . ,' said Kirsty, struggling to ask the

dreaded question. 'When are you going to send him away?'

He looked at her earnestly, knowing how she felt. 'In a day or two — when we're sure he's all right.'

'Where will you do it?'

'Near his old burrow — where you found him.'

'He'll be all alone.'

'Not at all. There'll be some other young fellows still in the colony, getting ready to leave. And lots of grown-ups. His own parents could still be there. They sometimes lay a second pair of eggs, especially if something has happened to the first two chicks.'

'Can we come — when you let him go?'

'Well, of course. We have to do it together, all three of us.'

'When?'

Dr Piper considered the point. 'What about next Wednesday?'

'What time?'

'In the evening, just before it gets dark. All the other penguins will be coming back from the day's fishing so there'll be plenty of company. He won't feel lonely.'

'I'll tell Mum,' said Kirsty. 'I'll say we might be late for tea.'

'Good,' answered Dr Piper. 'Do you think she'd like to come too — to meet Pinquo? She and your father.'

Kirsty and Tim both rollicked about at that.

'Mum doesn't like penguins,' said Tim, 'and Dad's too busy.'

Dr Piper didn't make any more comments. 'All right,' he said. 'Wednesday then.'

And so it was arranged. On Wednesday they would set Pinquo free — for ever.

6

On Wednesday morning Kirsty woke up feeling very sad. And things were no better during the day. Twice the teacher spoke sharply to her. 'Kirsty Kemp, what on earth's the matter with you? You're walking about in a dream.'

Kirsty nursed her sore heart. Tim was the only other person in the little classroom who knew and understood, and he didn't say anything because he was feeling miserable too.

After school their mother gave them an early tea. As she put the plates in front of them she looked keenly at Kirsty. 'Well, my girl, you've got a proper dose of the dumps, haven't you?'

Kirsty poked at the food with her fork. 'It's going to be sad without Pinquo,' she said. 'It's going to be very lonely.'

Her mother smiled kindly. 'Of course,' she said. 'It's always sad when you have to say goodbye to something.'

'Yes.'

'But it's no use being sentimental about it either. Life is full of comings and goings.'

'Yes.'

'And wild creatures are meant to be free. You know that.'

Kirsty nodded. It was all she could do, because her throat was choked up.

'Dr Piper is sad too,' Tim said. 'I can tell.'

His mother poured them each a drink.

'I'm sure he is. But he also knows what's best for penguins.'

When they'd finished eating they tidied up and put on their old jeans.

'Now don't be late,' their mother said. 'We don't want you running about on you own in the middle of the night.'

'No, Mum.'

'In fact, it's such a lovely evening that perhaps we'll come down to meet you — your father and I.'

Kirsty brightened up. 'Oh Mum, would you?'

'If we can shut up the workshop in time.'

'Please, Mum. Come straight down before it gets dark. Then you can meet Pinquo.'

'We'll see.'

Kirsty and Tim were both bright-eyed and excited. 'Please, Mum. He's beautiful. You have to see him before he goes.'

'I'll speak to your father.'

'There won't be another chance. We may never see him again.'

Their mother thumped them gently on the shoulders. 'All right, all right. If we can manage it we'll walk down to Dr Piper's place just before dusk.'

'Thanks, Mum. Thanks.'

They ran towards the front door.

'But don't be disappointed if we're late,' she called after them. 'Your father could be held up.'

'We'll wait,' they yelled back. 'We'll tell Dr Piper.'

They raced off down the street past the jetty and the curving shore of Sickle Bay. A few minutes later they were knocking on the door of the little house with the white picket fence.

Pinquo was full of life and energy. It was almost as if he knew that something special was about to happen. He stood near his box-burrow and made a yapping sound, like a puppy trying to bark. Then he stretched his flippers and cocked his head as if listening for answering yaps from the sandhills and rocky shores near by.

'Oh yes, he's a lively boy,' said Dr Piper. 'He thinks he's a film star.'

They went back inside while Dr Piper finished his tea. He was delighted to hear that Mr and Mrs Kemp might be coming down and so he took as long as he could over his meal so that Kirsty and Tim wouldn't get too impatient while they were waiting for their parents. As he was eating he talked about penguins and the way they lived together.

'They're wonderful little creatures,' he said. 'And really very clever. Like most birds and animals they can roam far away but always find their way back home again.'

'I s'pose they've lived here for hundreds of years,' said Tim.

'Thousands,' answered Dr Piper. He shook the teapot and then poured himself another cup. 'Long before white people came to Australia, and probably even long before black people came.' He paused, sipping quietly at his tea. 'There's even a legend about them — from the Aboriginal storytellers. Old Micky Mandulla told me about it long ago.'

Kirsty looked up quickly. She was always interested in stories. 'What does it say?'

Dr Piper finished his drink and pushed the cup away. 'Well,' he answered at last, 'It's one of those stories where the wild creatures warn the people and save their lives.'

'Like the geese that saved ancient Rome?'

'Not exactly. This story says the penguins saved the people from the sea.'

'How?'

'They suddenly left their burrows and hollows and nesting places and fled inland as if they were terrified of something.'

'All of them?'

'All of them together, rushing and stampeding. And the Aboriginal people could read the signs and knew that a great danger was coming, so they fled inland too.'

Kirsty was wide-eyed. 'And what happened?'

'The sea roared over the land. If they'd stayed by the shore they would all have been killed. Or so the legend says.'

'Was it a great storm or something?'

'Something like that, I guess. And so the Aboriginal songmen made a big corroboree about it, and handed down the story for hundreds of years.'

'But the penguins could have swum away — into the sea.'

'Not really. They would have been pounded

against the rocks or trapped in their burrows. The sand would have collapsed on top of them.'

Kirsty considered the point carefully. 'I suppose so,' she said doubtfully.

Dr Piper laughed. 'Remember that it's only a story,' he said. 'The details have been lost long ago.' He looked at the clock. 'I think we'd better get ready. The sun has set and we mustn't keep our guest waiting.'

They went out into the backyard where Dr Piper picked up Pinquo easily and gently as if he were a pet duck. Kirsty watched sadly. 'Can I hold him?' she asked.

'Of course.'

Dr Piper's house was close to the sea. The street in front of his picket fence was a dead end. It was really nothing but a dirt track that stopped short a few metres further on. And beyond the track there was a small wilderness of sedge and sandhill that ended abruptly at the rocky shoreline and the sea.

Pinquo sat in Kirsty's arms, gazing from side to side in surprise. Tim held open the picket gate and they all trooped out into the roadway.

'Now,' said Dr Piper, 'I wonder if your mother and fath . . .' Then he gave a happy exclamation. 'Ah, here they are now. What good timing!' He strode forward to meet Mr and Mrs Kemp as they came hurrying down past Mrs Hempel's tumbledown fence next door. They were pleased to see him.

'We've heard so much about this penguin,' Kirsty's mother said, 'that we thought we'd better see him before he sets off.'

Dr Piper was delighted. 'I'm so glad. Come over and meet him.'

For five minutes after that there was a constant babble of talk. Pinquo was patted on the head, tickled under the chin, and stared in the eye. He had his flipper examined from this side and that side. He had clicking noises made near his ear and he was given words of praise and encouragement. He put up with it all very well.

'Now,' said Dr Piper at last. 'It's time for the great moment.' He turned to Kirsty and Tim.

'You two had better lead the way. You know exactly where you found him.'

They trooped off in a human caterpillar across the sandhills towards the rocks of the foreshore — Kirsty in the lead, Tim and his mother next, and Dr Piper and his father in the rear.

'Here,' said Kirsty at last. 'This is the spot.'

'Just there,' Tim added, pointing to the cleft. 'He was lying under that rock. His burrow is just behind it.'

'All right,' said Dr Piper. 'Then this is where we set him free.'

Kirsty gave Pinquo a long hug. Then she knelt down and stood him gently in the hollow.

'Goodbye, Pinquo,' she said. 'Look after yourself.'

The others could tell that she had a lump in her throat.

For a while Pinquo stood quietly. Then he turned his head towards his own tail, pressed his bill against his preen gland, and combed some of the waxy fluid through his feathers.

'He's preening himself,' said Dr Piper. 'He's quite unconcerned.'

Kirsty's mother smiled. 'He's certainly in no hurry to rush off.'

Dr Piper peered about carefully among the hollows. 'I think his family have gone. The burrow seems to be empty.'

'Will that worry him?'

'No. He can look after himself. He'll probably follow them within a day or two.'

At last Pinquo turned and moved towards the entrance. He paused and glanced at them briefly like someone saying goodbye at the front door before going inside for the night. Then he was gone.

'What a gentle little fellow,' said Mr Kemp.

'Oh yes, he's a thorough gentleman,' Dr Piper answered.

'What now?' asked Mrs Kemp.

'He'll probably leave with all the others in the morning when they go out fishing. But I doubt if he'll come back tomorrow night.'

Mrs Kemp was really interested after all.

'What will he do?'

'He'll go off with all the youngsters — in the wide wide sea.'

Kirsty gazed at the entrance to the hollow where Pinquo had disappeared. It looked as empty as her own heart.

They all turned and picked their way back across the rocks in the gathering gloom. Down on the beach and among the sedge thickets they could hear the barking and yapping of the other penguins as they returned to their burrows at the end of the day's fishing.

'Just listen to them,' said Kirsty's mother.

Dr Piper paused. 'It's wonderful,' he said simply. 'The endless cycle of it. Life goes on.'

Kirsty said nothing. To her, life seemed to be very cruel. It was taking Pinquo away from her — perhaps for ever.

7

Early the next morning Kirsty ran down to the seashore and clambered over the rocks to Pinquo's burrow. Dawn was just breaking and she could hear the little penguins yapping as they gathered in pairs and groups among the thickets and rocky hollows. Then they started to move quickly and quietly across the beach to the water.

As she came over the low tumbledown cliff near Pinquo's home she was just in time to see a shadowy little figure scuttle off among the rocks towards the sea. Others were criss-crossing the sand all around it, and she found it hard to see clearly in the gloom. She had no idea whether the solitary penguin was Pinquo or not, but she waved her hand and called out loudly, 'Goodbye, Pinquo.'

The little figure paused for a second and looked back as if it had suddenly heard a familiar voice. Kirsty's heart leapt. 'It *is* Pinquo,' she said softly to herself. But then the figure turned, hurried down to the sea, and plunged into the waves that were breaking along the shore. A moment later he was gone.

Kirsty stood there silently for a long time.

Then at last she walked home slowly in the growing light until sunrise was trembling on the brink of the east. She didn't even call in at Dr Piper's house. She wanted to keep this moment all to herself.

And so the waiting began. Christmas came and went, the summer holidays passed with hot days and baking beaches, and the new school year seemed to bury Kirsty and Tim in projects and homework and busy daytime jobs. Gradually their memories of Pinquo grew dim. They saw very little of Dr Piper — a chance meeting in the grocer's shop after school, perhaps, or a distant wave on the beach at the week-end.

But when the end-of-term holidays came round again in May their interest quickened. The Fairy Penguins were starting to come back to start the new breeding season — at first just a few dribbling in here and there, but soon a stream of newcomers every day, and finally a flood of little figures hurrying up the beach and jostling about among all the old haunts and hollows. Soon the rocky nooks were all occupied again and dozens of paths crisscrossed the grass and sedge patches inland. Little mounds of fresh earth and sand showed where new burrows had been dug or old ones had been cleaned out. Each one was about a metre long, and ended in a hollowed-out nesting place lined with grass and leaves ready for the new-laid eggs and freshly hatched babies.

Kirsty and Tim ran down to Pinquo's hollow

every day during the holidays to see if he had returned, and even when school started again they usually stood watching in the evening dusk. Dr Piper came too, carrying a flashlight to check the deeper nooks. They often stood there, the three of them together, gazing intently into the gloom. The bustling life of the penguin colony was going on all around them — pairs of little lovers standing side by side, raising and lowering their flippers and singing their dreadful songs. They sounded like a hundred sick donkeys braying with rusty nails in their throats. But nowhere was there even a hint of a year-old penguin with a lopsided look and a kinky flipper.

By now a good many people in Sickle Bay knew about Pinquo. Apart from Mr and Mrs Kemp, and Mrs Hempel who lived next door to Dr Piper, most of the shopkeepers had heard the story and wanted to know if there was any news. Sometimes they had their facts mixed up, but they were interested just the same.

'How's that penguin of yours getting on?' they would ask. 'The one that got run over last year?' Or again, 'Has that pet Fairy turned up yet — the one with the broken leg?'

Only old Mrs Martin, the postmistress, was sour and suspicious. She stood behind the little counter with her scales and her stamp book, warning Kirsty about the terrible danger she was in.

'Don't touch birds or animals,' she said. 'Don't touch anything at all. And especially don't touch that penguin of yours.'

'Why not?' asked Kirsty innocently.

'They bite and scratch and they're covered in ticks and then they give you germs. If that penguin pecks your hand and draws blood you'll get tettnuss for sure.'

Kirsty was dumbfounded.

'There's no cure for tettnuss,' Mrs Martin went on. 'You just die.'

Luckily Kirsty always asked her mother and father about Mrs Martin's terrible warnings.

'Mum, what's tettnuss?'

'Tetanus, dear. It's an infectious disease.'

'Can you cure it?'

'It's best to prevent it — by having an anti-tetanus injection.'

'Could a penguin give it to you?'

Her mother raised her eyebrows. 'Perhaps. Who gave you that idea?'

'Old Mrs Martin.'

Kirsty's father laughed loud and long. 'Don't worry about Mrs Martin, love. Each morning when she wakes up she's amazed to find that she's still alive. She's forever afraid that all the germs of the world are going to swoop down in a cloud like huge mosquitoes and carry her away.'

May went by, and so did June and July. The cold winter winds swept in from the west and the seas raged white along the shore. They thundered against the underbelly of Kangaroo Island and the long curve of the Coorong coast. They hurled themselves against the rocky shore of Tasmania and towered through Bass Strait where the ships plunged and bucked and the oil rigs shuddered on their monstrous legs of steel.

But the little penguins were snug in their burrows, brooding warmly on their two white eggs. And there was still no sign of Pinquo.

One day when Kirsty was roaming along the shore, rugged up in her duffle coat and woollen pirate's cap, Dr Piper came striding over the sandhills towards her.

'Ohoo, Kirrrsty,' he called.

She paused. 'Hi,' she yelled into the wind.

He came up to her, panting hard. His face was redder than ever. His cheeks had been polished by the wind until they shone.

'Pinquo's burrow is occupied,' he said, 'but not by him. I thought you'd like to know.'

'Oh,' she said simply. 'By someone different?'

'By a breeding pair.'

He was silent for a while. 'They're probably Pinquo's parents. They usually go back to the same burrow.'

She thought about it for a while. 'Of course. He'd have to start a new burrow, wouldn't he? One of his own?'

'Yes.'

'It could be anywhere, couldn't it?'

'Yes, but almost certainly here somewhere — in this colony.'

She looked up at him earnestly.

'Do you really think he's here somewhere?'

'No I don't. He hasn't come back at all. Not this year.'

'Next year, then?'

'Perhaps. Or the year after that.'

She pulled the scarf more tightly around her neck.

'It's a long wait,' she said.

He smiled kindly. 'It's a cycle,' he answered. 'It takes its time. We have to wait.'

She was depressed. 'If something has happened to him it's a wait that could last for ever.'

8

On her eleventh birthday Kirsty's greatest wish came true. She was given a pony. She called it 'Captain', and for the next few months she spent every spare minute on its back, galloping over the countryside like a warrior. Her favourite spot was Baker's Knob, a little hillock behind the town, where she could sit in the saddle and look out over the whole of Sickle Bay and the curving coast beyond. It made her feel like a sentinel, a knight on watch against dragons and monsters.

Tim was not interested in horses. He didn't mind when Kirsty and some of her friends imagined they were leading the Charge of the Light Brigade because it left him free to roam about on his bike with Candle Light. Candle had such a long thin body and such startling red hair that his nickname was strangely proper. When he rode his bike up the seaside tracks with Tim his knobby knees kept rising and falling near the level of his ears so that he looked like a pedalling grasshopper.

Horses and bikes and homework kept Kirsty and Tim so busy that Pinquo almost faded from their minds. Another year ended and a new year started. Summer gave way to autumn, and autumn turned into winter. It was soon too wet for Kirsty to go galumphing about on Captain, and too wild for Tim to ride his cranky bike along the windswept tracks near the cliffs. But it was not too rough for the penguins to come home again to clean out their old burrows and to sit hunched in their nesting hollows, keeping the eggs snug against the warm flesh of the brood-patch under their bellies.

And so the time went by until one Sunday morning in September. Kirsty was padding about the kitchen in pyjamas and bare feet, making toast, and Tim was searching for a clean shirt. It was just half-past seven and their parents were still asleep. As Kirsty took the first round of toast from the toaster there was such a thunderous thumping at the front door that she dropped one of the pieces on the floor. In a flash Moggs, the cat, had rushed up and sniffed all over it.

'Oh, blow,' said Kirsty.

She turned and started up the passage towards the door but glanced down at her pyjamas and bare feet and checked herself.

'Tim,' she called. 'Answer the door.'

Tim's muffled voice came from his bedroom where he was pulling his shirt over his head.

'You go . . . I'm getting dressed.'

'I can't.'

'Why not?'

'I'm not dressed either.'

'Ahhh!'

There was another tremendous thump on the front door, followed by the rattling of the door-handle. Mrs Kemp's voice came down the passage angrily. 'Kirsty! Tim! For goodness sake answer the door.'

Tim came stomping out of his room with his shirt hanging loosely over his underpants. His bare legs stuck out from beneath it like matchsticks from a potato. He didn't seem to be concerned that he was not really dressed to receive visitors at the front door.

'I'm coming,' he yelled — more for his mother's benefit than the stranger's — and then went on muttering to himself. 'For Pete's sake, what time is it? Six o'clock?'

He reached the door, unclipped the latch, and pulled it open. Kirsty, standing tiptoe in the kitchen, and her mother listening tensely from her bed, heard the creak of the hinge. Then there was a moment's silence followed by the sound of Tim's voice, greatly astonished.

'Dr Piper!'

'Hullo, Tim.' It was a hasty greeting, urgent and loud.

'Gosh, we thought it was the police or the space invaders.'

Dr Piper was breathless. 'I'm sorry it's so early,' he said apologetically. 'But I couldn't wait.' He checked himself suddenly and laughed. 'Have I caught you without any pants on?'

Tim blushed. 'I was just getting dressed.'

As soon as she knew who the visitor was Kirsty slipped across the passage to her own

43

room and came out in her dressing-gown.

Dr Piper beamed at them both. His cheeks were rosy from the cold air and his shock of white hair looked as if it had been tousled by a whirlwind. His eyes were fairly dancing with excitement.

'I've got news for you,' he said. 'You'll never guess.'

Kirsty gave a shout. 'It's Pinquo! He's back?'

Dr Piper's grin was as wide as a slice of melon. 'Can you come and see?'

Kirsty did a jump and a skip in her bare feet. 'Yippee!'

'Can you come?' Dr Piper asked again. 'Can you come at once?' There was something in the tone of his voice that suddenly made Kirsty pause. 'It is Pinquo, isn't it? He is back?'

Dr Piper seemed to be hugging himself with delight. Instead of speaking he nodded his head so vigorously that his white hair bounced and trembled all ways at once.

'What else, then?'

It was clear that Dr Piper had a secret, and that they were going to have to see it for themselves.

'Can you come — straight away?'

Tim was getting impatient. The wind was swirling through the open doorway and getting under his shirt. Every now and then it billowed up around his waist. Standing there in his underpants he looked like a ballet dancer in a tutu.

'We'll have to get dressed,' he said. 'But it won't take a minute.'

Kirsty was already running back to her room. 'We'll be down at your place in ten minutes.'

Dr Piper was still smiling. 'I'll wait,' he called.

Tim was back in the blink of an eye and Kirsty wasn't far behind him. They were rugged up in jumpers and scarves and jeans and big woollen caps. Kirsty poked her head round the door of her parents' bedroom.

'Pinquo's back,' she said breathlessly. 'We're going down to see.'

Her mother rolled her eyes at the ceiling. 'So I've gathered,' she said weakly.

Her father opened one eye and tugged at the bedclothes. 'And don't slam the door,' he said. 'You're like a herd of elephants.'

Luckily Dr Piper didn't hear any of this. He was already at the front gate, leading the way. Once in the street he strode out so enthusiastically that even Kirsty had to trot beside him to keep up. They hurried down past the jetty, and skirted Mrs Hempel's fence.

'Is he back in his old burrow?' Kirsty asked, panting hard. 'Back in the rocks where we found him?'

Dr Piper hugged his secret to himself. 'You'll see,' he answered. 'You'll soon see.'

Kirsty was veering off across the roadway towards the beach but Dr Piper called her back. 'This way, this way.'

Tim looked up questioningly. 'In the sandhills, is he?'

'We thought he might do that, didn't we?' Kirsty said. 'We guessed he'd have to make a new home of his own.'

And then, quite suddenly Dr Piper turned in through his own picket gate and set off down the side of the house. 'This way,' he called.

Tim and Kirsty were astonished. 'Have you got him back in the yard?' Kirsty asked. There was an accusing tone in her voice. 'You haven't caged him up again, have you?'

Dr Piper put his finger to his lips as if to say, 'Shhhh,' and led the way down the path between the house and the paling fence. It was a narrow lane, no more than a metre wide, so they had to walk in single file with Dr Piper's head and shoulders bobbing along in the lead.

'Pinquo must be hurt,' Kirsty whispered to Tim. 'Dr Piper must have found him on the beach or in the rocks and brought him back here.'

'It's probably his flipper,' Tim whispered back. 'It must have packed up again.'

They reached the backyard and Dr Piper headed for the far corner, picking his way past a jumble of old boxes, cages, bits of roofing iron, fenceposts, stakes, and rolls of wire mesh. 'This way,' he said softly.

A wooden crate was lying upside down in the corner, its open side facing the ground and the strong boards of the bottom humped up in the air. It was almost a metre square. A lot of loose sand and dirt lying about in front of it as if a dog or a rabbit had been busily burrowing underneath the wooden edge to get at the little cave inside.

Dr Piper became more cautious than ever as

he approached the crate, bending his body and tiptoeing forward until he looked like a walking question-mark. He signalled to Kirsty and Tim, indicating that they should avoid the loose sand in front and come round to the side. There he pointed to a kind of peep-hole in the crate — partly a crack, partly a broken knot in the wood — and bent down to peer into it. A moment later he stood upright again with a huge grin on his face, nodding his head vigorously as if saying 'Yes, yes, yes' to a very important question.

Kirsty raised her eyebrows and pointed to the hole, and again Dr Piper nodded until his white hair danced. Kirsty stepped forward, bent down, and peered carefully into the crate. At first she couldn't see anything at all but as her eye grew accustomed to the gloom she slowly made out the form of a bird's head and shoulders, and eventually its whole body hunched in a nest of twigs and leaves and feathers. It was a Fairy Penguin.

She stood up, smiling, and Tim hurried forward to take her place.

'Is it Pinquo?' she whispered. Her eyes were bright with surprise and delight.

Dr Piper was even more excited than she was. 'Pinquo's wife,' he said, hugging himself.

Tim was vaguely disappointed. 'Where's Pinquo, then?'

'Fishing. He'll be back at dusk. You must come and meet him.'

Dr Piper led them away quietly, making for the house. 'Breakfast?' he asked.

Tim was always hungry. 'Yes, please,' he answered quickly. 'We haven't had time to eat anything yet.'

While they waited for the kettle to boil and the milk to heat Dr Piper told them his story. He was still as excited as a boy.

'I couldn't believe my eyes,' he kept saying. 'I just couldn't believe my eyes.'

'When did they come?' asked Kirsty.

'I don't know. I just don't know.'

'When did you first see them, then?'

'This morning.'

Tim was astonished. 'This morning?'

'Yes.'

'Early?'

'At first light. When Pinquo was just setting off to go fishing for the day.'

'Where?'

'Past my bedroom window.'

Kirsty almost fell off her chair with laughter. 'Past the window?'

'Yes. I was sitting up in bed dialling the news on my radio when I caught a glimpse of something moving outside. I ran to the front door and there he was, just going out through the gate.'

'And you knew he was Pinquo?'

'Instantly. The same droopy walk, the same kinky flipper.'

'Did you follow him?'

'No. He was mixing with all his friends on their way down to the beach. I didn't want to frighten them.'

'Did you guess about Mrs Pinquo?'

'Not at first. I thought perhaps he was just paying me a visit.'

'When did you find out about her?'

'About an hour later. I went out into the backyard to see if I could find out what Pinquo had been up to. I thought he might have left some footprints in the sand, or perhaps a feather in his old cage.'

'And what did you find?'

'I found the burrow under the crate. I couldn't miss it.'

'With Mrs Pinquo inside?'

'Yes.'

'They'd made their nest in there and you didn't know anything about it?'

'Not a thing. And it would have taken them a couple of days at least.' He grinned again. 'It goes to show that you don't know what's going on in your own backyard.'

'It shows that Pinquo trusted you,' said Tim. 'To come in through the front gate like that and waddle down the side of the house.'

'Yes, in a way.' Dr Piper adjusted the glasses on his nose. 'But it's not unusual, that sort of thing. There have been lots of times when Fairy Penguins have made their nests in barns and sheds.'

'Really?'

'Oh, yes. They've even gone into people's houses. Mrs Hempel found one exploring her back verandah last year. She met him face to face at the kitchen door.'

Kirsty laughed. 'I'll bet she got a shock.'

Dr Piper clutched his chest and imitated Mrs

Hempel. 'A real turn, it gave her. A real turn.'

They sat down at the breakfast table.

'Do you think Pinquo will still know us?' Tim asked, his mouth full of toast.

Dr Piper smiled. 'We'll know before long, won't we?'

'Tonight?'

'At dusk, when he returns.' He looked quizzically at Kirsty and Tim. 'You will come down again, won't you?'

They both nodded. 'We wouldn't miss it for the world,' Kirsty said.

9

Even Mr Kemp was surprised to hear about Pinquo. 'In the backyard?' he said, looking at Kirsty and Tim over the top of his Sunday newspaper. 'Good Lord!'

'Yes, under a big box,' Tim said eagerly. 'They didn't even have to dig out a nesting hollow — just a little burrow at the front door.'

'Under a box,' repeated his father. 'I like that. It shows a lot of labour-saving common sense.'

'We're going down just before sunset,' Kirsty said, 'to see Pinquo come home.'

Her mother looked at her with a kindly smile. 'Do you think Dr Piper would like us to watch too?'

'Yes, he'd love you to come. He said so.'

That was how it came about that Dr Piper's enclosed back verandah was like a crowded waiting-room that evening. During the day Candle Light and his brother had managed to invite themselves and at the last minute Mrs Hempel heard about it and asked whether she might come in with her niece, Belinda, from Melbourne.

Dr Piper's verandah was a very good observation point. A long row of small glass panes looked out over the backyard so that everyone could see what was going on, and there was a sliding window in the other wall facing the paling fence and the lane down the side of the house. By standing very close to it and pressing his left cheek against the glass Dr Piper could look down the lane and give warning of Pinquo's approach. And by opening the window and leaning out he could see right across the roadway to the sandhills and the curving shore. He left a light burning on the front verandah and another one at the back door. Kirsty was worried when she noticed this. 'They won't frighten Pinquo, will they?' she asked anxiously.

Dr Piper was unconcerned. 'Not with Mrs Pinquo at home in her nest. He'll come back to her. Nothing will stop him.'

As the shadows deepened everyone grew tense and excited. They talked in undertones, muttering senseless little comments and laughing in jerky spasms. Candle Light kept drilling at his right ear with his little finger and Mrs Hempel's niece giggled all the time. She was a spindly broomstick of a girl with pimples, and she kept nudging Kirsty and saying, 'Call me Sticky — it's short for stick insect'. Several times Dr Piper looked at her sourly. Kirsty knew that he didn't like giggling girls at the best of times, least of all at a moment like this.

Before long they could hear the evening sounds of the penguin colony — the yapping and braying of travellers returning and couples in love. Dr Piper was peering stealthily out of the side window, motioning the others with his hands, warning them to be silent and attentive.

'Here he comes,' he whispered suddenly. 'He's crossing the road to the gate.'

They all held their breaths.

'He's coming down the side of the house,' he whispered a moment later. Then he stood with his finger pressed to his lips, evidently watching as the little penguin passed right underneath the window. A moment later Pinquo entered the backyard and hurried down towards the nest in full view of all the watchers. When he reached the entrance burrow he paused, bent low as if peering inside for a moment, and then stood up and started preening himself. He was probably making little noises from time to time, but in the enclosed space of Dr Piper's verandah it was hard for the human listeners to hear.

Suddenly Pinquo's mate popped out of the nesting burrow and stood near by, stretching herself.

'Look, look,' said Dr Piper.

Pinquo seemed to approve of his wife very much. He began to raise and lower his flippers, at the same time singing his dreadful tuneless song. From time to time he lifted his head in the air and stared upwards in ecstasy. After a few moments his wife joined him in the flipper ballet and they spent a few minutes in blissful companionship. Then, in an instant, they both darted quickly into the burrow and

disappeared.

Stick Insect clapped her hands as if she had been watching a concert, and Candles said, 'Well, what d'you know!' The visitors thanked Dr Piper for allowing them to watch and then slowly went off home. As Kirsty and Tim walked past the jetty with their parents the ripples lapped gently on the shore and the moonlight lay across the bay in a glade of winking silver. Kirsty sighed contentedly. She had never been happier.

It was the beginning of a wonderful time for Dr Piper and the Kemp family. They watched the two little penguins constantly. Before long there were two white eggs in the nesting hollow under the crate, and the long process of incubating and hatching began.

'How long?' asked Tim.

'Five weeks,' answered Dr Piper. 'Thirty-five days, give or take a bit.'

'That's a long time,' Kirsty said.

Tim scoffed. 'An elephant takes nearly two years.'

'Sitting on an egg?' Kirsty shrieked with laughter.

Tim blushed. 'You know what I mean.'

Dr Piper took notes every day. He said that people didn't know nearly enough about the little penguins, and this was a splendid chance to study their lives without disturbing them.

'They are safe in my backyard,' he said. 'There are no idiots running about with guns, and no fools poking sticks into burrows. And there are no dogs or dingoes or foxes.'

After a week or two Dr Piper finally made himself known to Pinquo again. It was a Saturday evening and Kirsty and Tim had gone down to watch. Pinquo and his mate had been taking it turns to sit on the eggs, sometimes for a day or two, sometimes for a week or more at a time. And while the one crouched in the nest, pressing the eggs against the warm brood patch on its belly, the other went off to look for food. Dr Piper knew that Pinquo had gone out to fish, and so as evening fell he stood casually in the backyard near the old cage, waiting for his return. When he saw the penguin coming down the laneway beside the house he stepped forward slightly, made a clicking noise in his throat, and said, 'Hullo, Pinquo.'

The penguin stopped short and looked Dr Piper up and down. Kirsty and Tim watched breathlessly from the verandah. 'Hullo, Pinquo,' Dr Piper said again, and made the strange penguin sounds he had used when feeding the little bird long before.

Something stirred in Pinquo's memory. He took a step towards Dr Piper and raised his flippers.

'Look, look,' said Kirsty to Tim. 'He's saying hullo. And his flipper is still as droopy as ever.'

'And he's just as friendly.'

It was true. Dr Piper raised his hand very slowly and gently touched Pinquo under the chin. Instead of recoiling, Pinquo moved another step closer and lifted his head as if asking for more.

'He hasn't changed,' cried Kirsty. 'He's still warm and happy, just as he always was.'

Kirsty was right. Before long Pinquo was as tame as he had ever been. He waddled about the backyard as if he owned it, and sometimes even poked his head into the enclosed verandah while they were watching. He usually held his head on one side when he did that, as if asking whether they had seen anything interesting.

Pinquo's wife was much more aloof at first. This was only to be expected. However as time went by she was less and less concerned about the antics of human beings and didn't mind in the least if they constantly peered at her through the little peep-hole above her head. Kirsty called her Pinquette. Dr Piper said that such a name rather suggested that she was just a little Pinquo, but Kirsty was not persuaded. From that moment on, the two tenants in his backyard were Pinquo and Pinquette.

A few weeks later the two became four. Dr Piper was very excited. Exactly on the thirty-fourth day he announced that little piping sounds were coming from one of the eggs.

'The little fellow is cutting his way out,' he said to Kirsty and Tim that afternoon. 'He's cutting off the blunt end of the egg.'

Tim was amazed. 'From the inside?'

'Yes.'

'How on earth can he do that?'

'With a sharp point on the end of his bill. It's called an egg tooth.'

Kirsty was fascinated. 'That's wonderful,' she said. 'It's all worked out in advance, isn't it?'

'Yes, in the egg. Nature is always very wonderful,' Dr Piper answered. 'It'll take him a long time to chip his way out, but he'll do it.'

'How long?'

'A day or two. But both chicks will be out by the end of the week.' He chuckled. 'Then poor Pinquo and Pinquette are going to be worn to a frazzle.'

Tim looked up quickly. 'Bringing food for them?' Dr Piper nodded. 'Endlessly. The chicks will never be satisfied. They'll grow like mushrooms. In eight weeks they'll be ready to go to sea.'

For Kirsty and Tim the next month or two was the most interesting time of all. At first the two chicks were covered all over in fine down, except for a bare line down the belly where the brood patch was going to be. Their eyes were closed. Either Pinquo or Pinquette stayed on guard while the other one went fishing. Each night they exchanged their jobs.

After a few days the chicks were able to open their eyes and start crawling about in the nest. During the second week the first down was pushed out by a thicker coat, dark above and white below.

Kirsty was astonished at the speed of the change. She told the teacher about it, and before long arrangements had been made for all the children in the school to visit Dr Piper too. His backyard became a place for nature study lessons.

By now Pinquo and Pinquette both had to go fishing. They gathered up small fish and squid straight into their stomachs until they were bulging like balloons. Then they staggered up the beach and across the sand towards Dr Piper's place. Sometimes they were so overloaded that they stumbled and fell flat on their bellies.

'Poor Pinquo,' said Kirsty one evening when she was standing with Tim and her mother watching him. 'He's so loaded up that he can't quite manage it.'

'Now you see what parents do for their children,' her mother said wryly.

'Yes. They feed them fish and squid.' Tim answered cheekily.

Not content with waiting inside the nest for their parents the two chicks now came out of the burrow, begging food from any passing creature, including Dr Piper.

In the fifth week feathers began to show through the down, and the colour of the chicks' eyes changed to the blue-grey of their parents. By the seventh week the little penguins were almost fully grown, and a few days later they lost the downy ruff around their necks. They were now as big and heavy as adults — their bodies firm and nuggety, flippers strong, feathers gleaming white below and steel blue above.

One day towards the end of the eighth week Kirsty and Tim were down in Dr Piper's yard watching the chicks. They were almost as tame

as Pinquo now, following Dr Piper into the back verandah whenever he disappeared through the door.

'I've got a job for you today,' he said.

'What job?' they asked.

'Banding. I've decided to band them all — the chicks and Pinquo and Pinquette too.'

'Why?'

'To study them properly. Just to make sure there are no mistakes.'

'How do you band them?' asked Tim.

Kirsty knew. 'You put a ring around their leg — with a number and an address on it.'

'Not on their legs,' said Dr Piper. 'Not for penguins. You do use the legs for most other seabirds.'

Kirsty was surprised. 'What do you use for penguins?'

'A flipper.'

He pulled some bands from his pocket and held them up. 'See. They're flanged and shaped to fit around a flipper, up near the armpit. They're specially made for penguins.'

They sat down on a box. 'Now, you two can hold these young birds while I clip on the bands.'

He suddenly looked at Kirsty. 'You haven't named them yet have you? You'd better hurry. They'll be leaving soon.'

'I've been worrying about that,' she answered. 'I can't think of a good pair of names.'

'Pinto and Pintette,' suggested Tim.

'No. That would mix them up with Pinquo

and Pinquette.'

Tim pulled a face. 'Fisho and Fishette then,' he said.

Dr Piper roared. 'That's very good,' he said. 'They eat like it and they smell like it.'

'But are they a boy and a girl?' asked Kirsty.

'Yes, they are,' Dr Piper replied. 'The one with the deeper bill and the thicker head is a male. That's the only way you can tell.'

Kirsty looked at Tim with a glint in her eye. 'I should have known,' she said, 'that the males always have thicker heads.'

10

By the time Fisho and Fishette had gone off to sea it was late in December. Poor Pinquo and Pinquette looked skinny and worn out. Not long afterwards they disappeared.

Kirsty, whose daily chat with Pinquo had come to be an important part of her life, was very put out. 'Where are they?' she asked anxiously. 'Where have they gone?'

'They've gone to fatten up,' Dr Piper answered quietly. 'They'll be away for six or seven weeks, I should say. Then they'll come back to moult.'

'To what?'

'To moult. To lose all their feathers.'

'How horrible.'

'Not at all. They'll shed all the old ones and grow a beautiful coat of shining new ones.'

'How long will that take?'

'Three weeks.'

'What do they do while that's going on?'

'Nothing.'

'Don't they even eat?'

'No. They just sit in their burrows while the old feathers fall out and the new ones grow. They live on their fat.'

'For three whole weeks?'

'Yes. By the time it's over they've lost nearly half their weight.'

'I should think so.'

'So back they go to fatten up again — ready for the next breeding cycle.'

Kirsty smiled. They don't get much rest, do they?'

Dr Piper pushed his glasses more securely on to his nose. 'No. Nature works according to a stern plan. There's no place for slackers.'

Kirsty jumped down from the fence where she'd been sitting. 'Mum says there's no place for slackers in our house and I've got all my homework to do.'

Dr Piper grinned. 'Good,' he said. He stood watching her as she skipped up the road. 'I'll let you know,' he called, 'when Pinquo gets back.'

She turned and waved. She said something too, but her voice was thin and piping like a seagull's cry lost on the sea wind. A moment later she was gone.

Now the great cycle of the seasons rolled steadily and rhythmically over the life of Sickle Bay. Pinquo and his mate came and went exactly as Dr Piper had said they would. They fattened themselves and moulted, fattened themselves again and returned for the new breeding season — under the same box in Dr Piper's backyard. They danced their love dance in the evening and Pinquo slapped Pinquette on the back with his good flipper and sang his song. They both took turns at sitting on their two white eggs until they had hatched, and eight weeks later a new pair of Fairy Penguins set off on their life's adventure in the great ocean.

Two more years went by. Kirsty turned fifteen. She was tall and supple, and her mother said she was growing faster than a pine tree. Candle Light thought she was beautiful. Tim was shorter and more chunky but he was growing quickly too. They were both going to high school. Every morning they caught the yellow school bus that lurched and grunted over the pot-holes for ten kilometres to Spoonbill Lake, and every afternoon they rode in it uncomfortably while it grunted and lurched its way home again.

They still had time to visit Dr Piper, especially during the summer months and in the school holidays, and they knew all about the comings and goings of the penguins. Whenever they saw Dr Piper hurrying up the street towards their front gate with his hair blowing and his face shining they knew that he was bringing some fresh news. By now Pinquo was so tame that he behaved as if he owned the house with the white picket fence. If the doors were open he was likely to waddle into the sitting room while Dr Piper was having a drink with his visitors. After looking them over he would examine the bedroom and the kitchen, have a quick peep at the laundry, and then wander out casually into the backyard again.

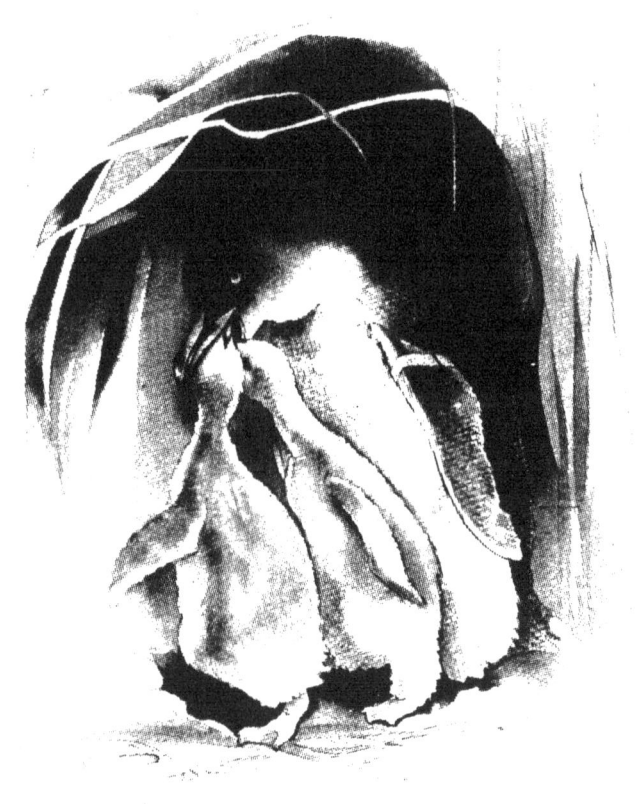

One Saturday morning shortly after Kirsty's fifteenth birthday Dr Piper came thumping on the door in great excitement.

'Can you come?' he cried as soon as Tim had answered his knock. 'Can you come down quickly?'

Kirsty hurried up beside Tim. 'What's happened?' she asked.

'I've got something to show you.'

'What is it this time?' asked Tim.

Dr Piper smiled happily. 'It's a real surprise.'

Kirsty and Tim both knew that Dr Piper would never tell them his secret unless they agreed to come.

'All right,' they said.

When they reached his house he led the way into the backyard as they had expected. But instead of making for the corner where Pinquo and Pinquette always made their nest he turned off towards the right, picked his way past an old bathtub and a heap of broken bricks, and stopped where a sheet of galvanised iron was lying against the paling fence. At his feet there was a tell-tale mound of loose sand and loam and beyond that the mouth of a new burrow. He took a torch from his pocket, crawled forward on hands and knees, and shone the torch beam into the hollow.

'Look,' he said.

They crouched down, peering forward with their cheeks against the sand. Less than a metre inside the burrow a penguin was crouching, blinking and looking a little sheepish. Kirsty caught a glimpse of a shining band on its flipper. She sat back in surprise.

'Not Pinquo?' she asked.

Dr Piper shook his head, grinning hugely. 'Fisho,' he said. Kirsty and Tim were both delighted. 'Fisho,' cried Kirsty. 'So he and Fishette have come back too — to their old home?'

'Only Fisho. The male usually arrives first to make the nest. His wife will be along shortly.'

Tim was fascinated. 'But what about Fishette?'

'She'll be somewhere else — with a husband of her own.'

Kirsty smiled. 'She might bring him back here too. You could finish up with a whole yard full of penguins.'

'Gosh,' said Tim, 'in years to come you'll be overrun.'

'Perhaps. But I won't mind. They're like little people.'

By now the story of Dr Piper's penguins was known far and wide. Tourists stopped and photographers wanted pictures.

Dr Piper joked about it to Kirsty and Tim. 'At this rate,' he said, 'the penguins will be more important than the people. Pinquo will be the most famous citizen of Sickle Bay.'

Dr Piper didn't know how true his prophecy was going to be.

11

Years afterwards people came to call it the Day of the Penguins. Nobody could ever remember all the details, except that it was a time of panic and confusion.

It began as a beautiful Sunday in spring — calm, peaceful, and sunny. In the middle of the afternoon Kirsty and Tim went to visit Dr Piper and they were soon sitting in his kitchen, waiting as usual for the kettle to boil.

Kirsty knew that she had learnt a great deal during the five years or more since she and Tim had first found Pinquo and carried him up to Dr Piper for help. She realised with a shock that while she and Tim were five years older and stronger, Dr Piper was five years older and weaker. His step was no longer as certain as it had been. He often seemed to be out of breath and his hand shook a little as he spooned the sugar into the cups. But he was happy and excited because the penguins were back and his backyard was a busier place than ever.

They were talking about the future. Dr Piper was worried because more and more campers and visitors and tourists were coming to Sickle Bay, littering the beaches and disturbing the penguins. They poked sticks into the rocky hollows and broke down the roofs of the burrows with their big feet. Whether it happened purposely or accidentally didn't matter — the damage was done all the same. As there were always some penguins in the colony, even in the off season, they were being molested more and more.

But today Sickle Bay was asleep. It was not a lively town at any time, and Sunday was the dreamiest day of the week. Three or four boys were sitting lazily on the jetty and a couple of dinghies were anchored out in the bay. One held two figures with lines in their hands, the other a lone fisherman lolling back with his hat over his eyes.

The main street was bare except for two cars parked in front of the Commercial Hotel.

'You could shoot a cannonball up the street in this town,' Mr Kemp always said, 'and all you'd hit would be the blowflies.'

Mrs Martin was in her little garden behind the post office, picking a few stunted flowers for the dining-room table because Mrs Hempel was coming to tea. Kirsty's horse, Captain, was standing in the far corner of his paddock flicking the flies with his tail. The penguins that had stayed behind crouched snugly in their nesting burrows waiting for their companions to return. Kirsty looked out of the window. 'What a lovely afternoon. Even the white caps have gone to sleep.'

She picked up the cups and took them over to the sink. 'I think we'd better go soon,' she said to Tim. 'What's the time?'

Tim looked at his watch. 'Almost five o'clock.'

And at that moment, as if it had been waiting for Tim's signal the world around Sickle Bay suddenly went mad. It began with a roaring sound that rushed towards them like a jet plane — a thunderous, tearing sound unlike anything they had ever heard before. An instant later the whole house shook violently as if a giant had seized it between his hands and was trying to rattle the windows out of it. At the same time the floor trembled under their feet and the furniture danced. The milk jug fell from the table with a crash and a row of dinner plates standing neatly on their edges on a shelf in the kitchen dresser fell forwards on their faces. Three of them broke into pieces. Kirsty, Tim, and Dr Piper were surrounded by the din of things rattling and crashing everywhere.

For a moment they were stunned. Kirsty stood clutching the sink so hard that the knuckles stood out white on the back of her hand. She was like a sailor clinging to a ship suddenly struck by a typhoon. Tim sat on his trembling chair, wide-eyed and white-faced. Dr Piper was the first to move. He leapt to his feet while the sounds still echoed about them and lunged at Kirsty, pushing her towards the door.

'Earthquake,' he yelled. 'Outside, quick!'

Tim sprang up as if he'd been stung. 'Earthquake,' he echoed. 'Holy catfish!'

They rushed frantically through the lounge

room and tumbled out of the front door on to the road. Dr Piper's white hair was standing up as if it had been charged with electricity. He was breathing heavily, whether from exertion or alarm Kirsty didn't know. The rumbling roar was still in the air but it had left the bay and seemed to be racing away to the north, dissipating its monstrous energy among the swamps and sandhills far inland. The earth still trembled a little — small, recurring vibrations as if the firm rock beneath their feet were still shuddering at what had just happened.

Dr Piper stood gazing about in astonishment.

'A quake,' he repeated. 'A big one.'

For a moment or two there was an uncanny silence in the world around them. The frogs in the swamps where there was normally pandemonium were deathly still. No plover called, no seabird cried. Even the calves and lambs were quiet, as if shocked and numbed.

Kirsty and Tim were more terrified than they cared to admit. There was something horrifying about the feeling of insecurity that had swept over them. The firm earth under their feet that was always so stable and enduring, so permanent and unshakable, had suddenly turn to jelly. And with it the whole universe seemed to have tumbled. They were frightened. They wanted to run away to escape from the shaking ground, to jump off, but there was nowhere to jump to, nowhere else to stand.

'It . . . it was a quake all right,' Tim said

uneasily at last. 'A really big one.'

And now a new wave of sound swept over the little town. It came from the people. Everywhere doors crashed open and gates were flung wide as the whole population of Sickle Bay tumbled out into the street. At the hotel a small group stood gaping at the two motor cars half buried under a tonne of bricks and blocks of limestone that had come hurtling down from the parapet above. The post office chimney had toppled on to the verandah in front of it, buckling the sheets of galvanised iron and denting part of the near-by roof. The smart white canvas awning above the entrance to the baker's shop, newly erected for the coming summer, was bowed down by a barrowload of rubble from the wall above. The big sign above the Kemps' petrol station was drooping drunkenly where one of the brackets had given way. Everywhere walls were cracked, poles askew, tanks leaking.

Dr Piper hurried into Mrs Hempel's place next door. 'Are you all right in there?' he shouted. Mrs Hempel appeared at the door, shaken and tottery. 'Was it an earthquake?' she asked.

'Yes, quite a big one.'

'I was just getting ready to go up to Vera Martin's place.' Kirsty took her arm. 'We'll take you there,' she said quietly.

Dr Piper agreed. 'And I think we should all stay outside for a while. There could be more to come — aftershocks.'

For almost an hour Sickle Bay remained in

uproar. People swarmed about on ladders, pushing down unsafe bricks and sweeping rubble and debris from verandahs. The owners of the two cars at the hotel gradually cleared away the mess of fallen masonry and exposed the crushed hoods and buckled bonnets. Tim and his father bolted a temporary bracket on to their garage hoarding to prevent it from falling down accidentally and killing someone. And all the while everybody listened, alert and tense, lest another shock should come roaring in on the town, bringing down whole walls this time and burying its victims in the ruins.

Charlie Hilbig, the publican, stood in the middle of the street talking to Dr Piper and Kirsty and her mother. 'I don't know whether to go back inside or not,' he said. 'It's almost tea time, and my guests have to be fed.'

Kirsty's mother smiled wryly. 'So does my family.'

Charlie turned to Dr Piper. 'Is it safe, do you think?'

Dr Piper shrugged. 'There could be aftershocks.'

Charlie pursed his lips. 'That's a risk we'll have to take sooner or later. Even if we stay outside we'll have to go in to get food and blankets.' He moved off uncertainly. 'I think I'll give it a try.'

Kirsty's mother looked out over the bay. A couple of fishing boats had hastily tied up at the jetty and their owners were hurrying up towards the town.

'It was a big shake,' she said. 'The worst in

living memory.'

Dr Piper nodded. 'If it had been a bit stronger there would have been a catastrophe.'

Kirsty gazed far across the land towards the hazy horizon. 'What about some of the other places down the coast?' she said. 'I wonder how they got on?'

'That depends on where the epicentre was,' said Dr Piper.

'Is that where the quake would have started from?'

'Yes.'

'Where do you think it was?'

'Probably out at sea somewhere — in Bass Strait, off the coast of Tasmania, along some old fault line. It could have been hundreds of kilometres away.'

Kirsty's mother was silent for a while. 'We're lucky that we don't have more big shocks like that,' she said at last. 'This used to be an active earthquake region, didn't it?'

Dr Piper nodded. 'Oh yes. Not so very long ago volcanoes were boiling and belching all the way from Mount Gambier to the middle of Victoria. There was molten lava all over the place.'

Kirsty shuddered. 'Let's hope it never happens again.'

They watched as the two fishermen ran up to the back gates of their houses. 'I wonder if the jetty has been damaged,' Kirsty said suddenly.

Dr Piper shook his head. 'Nothing more than a shake-up I should think. The sea wall and the cliffs are probably worse off — from falling rocks and so forth.'

Kirsty turned to him, suddenly alarmed. 'You don't think the penguins' burrows would have collapsed, do you — on to the nesting parents and babies.'

He reassured her. 'I doubt it'.

'But one or two of them could have been trapped by falling stones — just as Pinquo was?'

He smiled. 'Well, maybe.'

'I think we should go down and listen. We would hear them crying out.'

Her mother put out her hand and tousled Kirsty's hair. 'You can do what you like. I'm going inside to prepare something for tea.'

Kirsty looked up at Dr Piper. 'We should check, shouldn't we? Just in case. It'll be dark soon.'

He smiled again. 'Yes, I suppose we should.'

They were just hurrying down past the jetty towards Mrs Hempel's house when Kirsty stopped short and seized Dr Piper's arm. 'Look,' she cried, 'look, look!'

Dr Piper stopped abruptly and then had to readjust his glasses. 'Good Lord!' he said, dumbfounded. 'What on earth is happening?'

12

Pinquo had gone berserk. Whether or not he had just come home from a day's fishing they couldn't tell, but he was carrying on as he had never done before. First he rushed down the side of Dr Piper's house into the backyard. A few moments later he came hurtling back, shepherding Pinquette and Fisho in front of him, together with a couple of other penguin pairs that had recently adopted the place as their home.

He was like a creature possessed. Throughout the panic, as he was herding his family together, he seemed to be issuing orders and sending messages — yapping, crying, gurgling in a frenzy as if his life depended on it. When he had rounded up his relatives he left them standing momentarily near the front gate and rushed off across the sandy sedge-patch towards the beach, yapping and babbling like a maniac. Droves of other penguins were answering him on all sides. Their cries seemed to be just as urgent, just as passionate. Dozens were streaming up out of the sea now, even though it was much too early for their normal home-coming. They came scuttling up the sand in such desperate haste that they were colliding, falling on their faces, leaping up and rushing forwards again as if pursued by all the demons in the world.

Pinquo leapt and dashed about among them like a dervish, yapping and yabbering in a greater frenzy than ever. All round him a pandemonium of answering cries rose up until the air was filled with such a din that Kirsty held her hands to her ears. Suddenly he dashed up to the spot where she and Dr Piper were standing. He came at such a pace that he cannoned into her shin. She leapt back with a yell, but before she had recovered her balance he had rushed round her two or three times like a dwarf weaving a spell, stopped momentarily in front of Dr Piper with a gabble of yaps as if passing on a message of the most desperate and overwhelming importance, and then raced off again. But this time, instead of bursting his way back through the others towards the sea, he gathered up his family and shot off towards the jetty.

The others followed. In pairs and groups, in lines and streams, past rocks and sedges they came hurrying headlong until they emerged on to the open roadway past Dr Piper's white picket fence and Mrs Hempel's sagging gate. They were like an army of little soldiers racing to charge the enemy. In an instant Kirsty and Dr Piper were engulfed by them. Their shoes and shins were buffeted by a steel-blue sea, a rippling wave of heads and backs and flippers that surged on irresistibly, sweeping past them like a flood flinging itself round posts or pylons.

'Good Lord,' said Dr Piper again, holding on to his glasses for fear that they were going to be jolted from his nose and trampled underfoot.

Kirsty was beside herself. 'What's happening?' she cried. 'What on earth is going on?'

'There must be a thousand of them,' said Dr Piper in a daze. 'The whole colony. Every last one.'

'Look,' shouted Kirsty. 'They're heading for the town.' She yelled her disbelief. *'They're going up the main street!'*

Now other noises and cries came back to them above the sounds of the stampeding penguins. The townspeople were caught up in the ruckus just as Kirsty and Dr Piper had been. There were yells of 'Look out' and 'What's up'. Shrieks, exclamations, and anxious shouts echoed everywhere.

'There must be a reason,' said Dr Piper, looking over the top of his glasses in amazement. 'It's not normal behaviour.'

In spite of all the drama around them, Kirsty laughed. 'No,' she said, 'it's not.'

'It's too early in the day for them to come ashore,' he said. 'And they never dash off inland like that.'

'But where are they going?' asked Kirsty. 'For heaven's sake.'

The penguins were nearing the far end of the main street — a rippling mass that looked for all the world like a flock of little sheep. They were still being led by a single penguin — a small figure at the head of a family cluster that was in the van of the main army. Pinquo.

At the end of the street they veered left and pressed up the slope towards the higher ground.

'Baker's Knob,' cried Kirsty. 'They're heading for Baker's Knob.'

'For the high ground,' he said.

They both paused and looked at one another with wide eyes.

'The legend,' Kirsty cried breathlessly. 'The legend of the Aboriginal people. The story of the fleeing penguins.'

He spun round. 'It's a warning. A warning of great danger.'

Then he seized her arm and ran forward. 'Quick,' he cried. She hesitated uncertainly but he pulled her so hard that he almost lifted her from the ground. 'Run,' he shouted. 'Run for your life.'

For an old man he moved with astonishing speed. 'Why didn't I think of it before?' he kept saying, 'Why didn't I *think*?'

They raced past the jetty and came pounding up towards the hotel. He was straining hard and wheezing, constantly looking back over his right shoulder towards the sea. He burst in through the hotel door, panting desperately and shouted at the top of his voice. 'Run! Run for your lives!'

Charlie Hilbig's head popped out round the dining-room door. 'What's that?' he asked in alarm.

'Get out, get out,' yelled Dr Piper. 'Get everybody out. You've only got a few minutes. Maybe only a few seconds.'

Charlie's head jolted in fright. 'Where to?'

'The high ground. Baker's Knob. Follow the penguins.'

Dr Piper raced out with Kirsty. 'Run ahead,' he cried. 'Warn everyone. Tell them to hurry, hurry, hurry! There's a tidal wave coming!'

He ran up to the next house where Bernie Williams lived with his grown-up son, Sam. Bernie was a fisherman so he didn't have to hear the warning twice. 'Get Mrs Martin,' gasped Dr Piper. 'And old Mrs Hempel. They're having tea together.'

'But they can't walk very fast,' answered Bernie.

'Grab them. Grab them and carry them. Piggyback them up the street if you have to. Take them to Baker's Knob.'

'Crikey,' said Bernie, picturing himself with old Mrs Martin on his back.

Luckily most of the people who lived along the street were still standing outside, buzzing with astonishment at the sight of the penguins.

'Tidal wave coming,' yelled Dr Piper, almost at his last gasp. 'Head for Baker's Knob. Follow the penguins.'

At last the cry was taken up by everyone else. 'Follow the penguins! Follow the penguins!'

'Hurry, hurry,' cried Dr Piper. 'Warn everyone. Hammer on the windows. Break down the doors. Get all the people out.'

Men and women came running from all sides, carrying their small children, hustling the old people along.

'Quick, quick,' urged poor Dr Piper, whose voice by now was little more than a croak.

Tim's father was running up the street, pushing Grandpa Klomp's wheelchair ahead of him at breakneck speed. The old man was clapping and laughing. 'Whee,' he piped. 'We're winning the race.' Tim was helping his mother with a basket of food and a jerry can of water. 'Quick, Mum,' he yelled. 'We haven't got time for all this.'

It was an unbelievable sight. On the crest of Baker's Knob a thousand penguins were converging into a tight flock, rounded up not by a sheepdog but by a penguin with a drooping flipper. Below them on the slopes of the knoll came the people of the town — every man, woman, and child in Sickle Bay — straggling and panting as they made good their ground. And behind them came Dr Piper, staggering and exhausted.

'How do you know?' Charlie Hilbig called out to him. 'How did you find out?'

Dr Piper was almost too faint to answer. He lifted his hand and pointed at the penguins, especially the small figure that still seemed to be in command.

'The penguins,' he gasped. 'The penguins. Especially Pinquo.'

The land lay in shadow now. Only out at sea where the plain of water stretched far away towards the southern horizon was there still a sheen of light and steely colour.

As the last of the fleeing townspeople struggled up Baker's Knob they milled about uncertainly. There was a great deal of noise. The penguins were still yapping in a frenzy and the people were worse.

Dr Piper began to regain his breath and looked about for Pinquo. Tim's father locked the wheels of Grandpa Klomp's wheelchair to make sure that it couldn't go charging back down the hill on its own. Tim dropped his mother's basket gratefully. He wondered vaguely whether the whole thing was a false alarm or a big practical joke.

And then, abruptly, the noise of the penguins ceased. It was as sudden as the slamming of a door. The people paused in amazement and were silent too.

'Look,' said Tim's mother breathlessly, pointing out over the little town at their feet towards the bay and the open coastline beyond. 'Look at the sea.'

A dozen awestruck voices took up the cry. 'Look at the sea. Look at the sea.'

'Holy catfish,' murmured Mr Kemp.

'Good Lord,' said Dr Piper for the fifth time that day.

The sea was draining away. It was drawing back from the coast as if a giant vacuum cleaner were sucking it out into the deeps of the ocean. The sea bay seemed to be emptying before their eyes. The water was sweeping out through the entrance like a mill-race, a turbulent rip of foam and whipping spray.

Large arcs of sand began to grow beyond the beach and long sandbanks appeared in the middle of the bay. Fish, unaware of the sudden retreat of the water were caught arching and flapping on dry land. Crabs scuttled about frantically.

'What's happening?' asked Tim. 'What on earth is happening?'

His father suddenly pointed. 'Look at the penguins.'

Tim looked around hastily. Every penguin had turned and was facing the ocean as if waiting for some kraken or penguin god to rise up out of the water.

'It's coming,' said Dr Piper softly. 'Look. Look.'

And now a great wall of water stood up sharply out of the sea. It seemed to come from nowhere, as if by magic. They barely had time to blink before they realised that it was travelling towards them at a tremendous speed.

The penguins all leant forward, their eyes glistening and their heads cocked sideways in an attitude of intense concentration. It was as if they recognised the arrival of the monster whose coming they had sensed long before. They were quite silent. The people were silent too. They stood rigid, awestruck, every gaze fixed on the sea below.

The wall of water came racing towards the outer entrance of the bay. They could see it clearly now, a vast bank nine or ten metres high, stretching away endlessly up and down the coast — millions and millions of tonnes of water sweeping towards them at the speed of a racing car.

It reached the outer edges of the bay where the low headlands curved out in a rocky reef towards the entrance. But there was no pause. It rolled over the entrance and stormed across the headlands as if they were pimples of sand and stone. In the same instant the flanks of the bank reached the shoreline beyond the bay — the low rocky buttresses and the sandy hummocks where the penguins had made their burrows.

There was a violent convulsion. Great plumes of water shot high into the air and tongues of spray lashed about them like lightning. But the bank rushed onwards unchecked, drowning the humps of rock, swallowing the sandhills and salty flats, wolfing up the sedge-patches in front of Dr Piper's house.

And then at last they heard it — at first a long low rumble like thunder in the distance. But it grew and grew like the sound of a thousand jet planes hurtling down upon them until it reached such an unbelievable crescendo that the people winced or put their hands over their ears to shut out the hurt. The roar and the wave seemed to rush at them together. The air and the ground shook. It was another earthquake, an earthquake of water.

And now it rushed down on Dr Piper's house. For a second the picture held there like a frame frozen on a television set — the white picket fence, the painted weatherboard walls, the brick chimney, and the untidy backyard

filled with boxes and crates and cages where Pinquo and his friends still lived. From the top of Baker's Knob it looked like a doll's house. And then it was gone.

The tidal wave roared over it at a hundred kilometres an hour.

'Oh my God,' said Dr Piper softly.

All around him the other people were standing stunned, spellbound, their ears still numbed by the monstrous roar of the water. Bits of the house shot up like flotsam in a hurricane — a wall-panel, a glinting piece of glass from a window, a couple of shattered rafters catapulted out as violently as debris from an explosion. Foam and spray seethed about in the maelstrom. Mrs Hempel's house disappeared too, in the same fearful instant, not even a chimney brick of the stub of an old fencepost remaining when the fury was finally over.

At the head of the bay the wave thundered over the jetty, wrenched off a long slab of decking and sent it hurtling end over end like the tray of a somersaulting truck. The old railway lines that were used to trundle the fish trollies up and down from the boats were torn off and twisted around the jetty piles like liquorice. The leading edge of the wave looked like the Niagara Falls — a cliff of leaping water. The two cars in the street were picked up and hurled about like ping-pong balls.

The Commercial Hotel was the only two-storey place in Sickle Bay. It was a big square building, with thick walls of limestone and a wooden balcony all the way around it about four metres above the ground. The tidal wave struck it like a pile-driver. In a flash the balcony had been wrenched off, and the outbuildings in the yard had been tumbled over and over and pounded to bits. The windows disappeared and the rooms were filled with water. But the building stood. Although the walls shuddered and the roof creaked the four-square old hotel emerged like a battle-scarred fort standing waist-deep in water.

A second later the lower part of the town was engulfed as well — Mr Harper's bakery, the café and grocery store, Mrs Martin's post office, and all the low-lying houses. Some were swept away altogether, some left in ruins with walls pushed in and roofs dumped in the street, some merely flooded to the windowsills. But as the street sloped upwards towards Baker's Knob, the more distant shops and houses began to escape the flood.

The monstrous wave of water was steered at last by the shape of the land. Leaving the higher part of the town untouched it swept round the slopes of the hill and roared inland over the low-lying swamps and flats. Captain's paddock was drowned in a flash, and so were the summer pastures beyond. But slowly the impetus died. The water grew shallower and shallower and lost its speed. Soon it was no more than two metres deep, and then one metre, and then fifty centimetres — seething round the fenceposts, bickering among the granite outcrops, licking the limestone. The noise died as its strength subsided.

Almost at once the water began to drain away again, carrying with it many of the things it had destroyed, leaving them stranded sadly along the line that marked the high point of its fury. Before long most of the town was clear of the sea.

Now at last the people could speak again. They were still aghast. Charlie Hilbig came over to Dr Piper. 'You saved our lives,' he said.

Dr Piper shook his head. 'I didn't. It was Pinquo. Pinquo and the penguins.'

'I wouldn't have believed it,' Charlie said. 'Was it the earthquake that caused it?'

Dr Piper nodded. 'Out at sea somewhere. Probably hundreds of kilometres away.'

'I had no idea a tidal wave could move so fast.' Charlie looked around. 'Well, I'd better go down and see what's left of my place.'

'Wait,' said Dr Piper. 'There could be more. There could be aftershocks.'

'Really?'

'Yes.'

'How are we going to know?'

'The penguins will tell us. Just watch them.'

Dr Piper was right. The sea heaved and rolled uneasily for a while and twice a long bank of water surged across the bay in a mini tidal wave. But that was all. As the dusk deepened and the moon rose, the penguins suddenly yapped quietly among themselves and then started to move off down the hill. The leader paused for a moment where Dr Piper and Tim and Kirsty were standing as if to say, 'It's all clear.'

'Is that you, Pinquo?' Kirsty asked excitedly as she peered forward in the gloom.

'That's Pinquo,' said Dr Piper. He made a singing penguin noise at the back of his throat. The penguin raised his flippers and did a quick waddle around all three of them in a kind of salute. Then he charged off down the hill at the head of his flock, leading them back to the rocky hollows and flooded burrows near the shore.

'Poor Pinquo,' said Dr Piper. 'His house is probably ruined as completely as mine.'

Everybody started to make hasty arrangements for the night. Those whose houses were still standing offered to take in those whose houses were not. Luckily the weather was fine and warm and so some people could sleep outside if they wanted to.

'You're coming with us,' Kirsty's mother said to Dr Piper. 'I think our place is safe.'

'It was saved by a whisker,' Mr Kemp said. 'The water looked in at the front door and then went away again.'

There was no electricity so they had to eat by candlelight.

Kirsty's father looked at Dr Piper over the candle flame. 'How on earth did you know?' he asked. 'About the stampede of the penguins? How did you know what it meant?'

Dr Piper glanced at Kirsty. They both smiled. 'It's a very old story,' he answered quietly.

'It's a miracle, really,' said Kirsty's mother.

'Dear old Pinquo. He deserves a medal.'

Tim laughed. 'Around his neck? He wouldn't like that. A band on his flipper is bad enough.'

Kirsty's mother sighed. 'Well, I hope that at least he can go on living a happy life now — for many more years.'

The others agreed.

But none of them knew what was about to happen.

13

At about the time Pinquo and the penguins started their stampede up the main street of Sickle Bay a big ship was nosing its way up the coast five or six kilometres out to sea. It was a tanker called the *Petro Queen*, and it was loaded down with almost a hundred-thousand tonnes of oil. From the bridge the captain could look out over the low flat deck stretching on and on ahead of him towards the bow. It was as long as a football field — a vast tank divided into sections so that from above it looked something like a huge log cake that had been cut into slices.

The weather was strangely perfect. Some of the crew were lounging in the last rays of the afternoon sun. Others were resting down below before beginning the night watch. The cook was busy in the galley making dumplings. A little while earlier the radio operator had come to the captain with a news item about an earthquake that had rattled the mainland, and one or two crewmen were listening to their radios to see whether it had affected their home towns. There was no mention of tidal waves. There was no thought of danger.

And so the *Petro Queen* had very little warning. The captain was just bending down to pick up a pen from the floor when the look-out gave a yell. The captain straightened up with such a start that he hit his head on the edge of the chart table and stood bewildered for a second or two, rubbing his temple and glancing quickly from side to side. The look-out was pointing madly and shouting 'Look, look!'

'Oh my God!'

'It's a wave. A freak wave.'

'A tidal wave.'

The captain collected his senses and bellowed at the helmsman. 'Port, port! Ninety degrees port.'

It was too late. The ship was as ponderous as a waterlogged tree trunk and answered far too slowly. In any case the tidal wave bore down with such power and fury that any manoeuvre was useless. It roared over the ship, dumping hundreds of tonnes of water on the deck, smashing every pane of glass on the bridge, flooding the galley and the crew's quarters and the engine room. At the same time it lifted the whole tanker from below, heaving it up amidships like a weight-lifter hoisting a barbell.

For one unbelievable moment the ship was actually balanced like a seasaw on a huge mound of water with the stern and the bow hanging in mid-air on either side. Then there was a hideous wrenching of welded steel plates as the great vessel broke its back and split in two. The bow section rolled over and sank at once, but the stern section miraculously survived.

It was all over in a minute. The tidal wave hurtled shorewards and the stern was left bobbing in the aftershocks, listing perilously and looking rather like a lunatic houseboat. But it was still afloat and for the moment the captain and a dozen crewmen were safe. Unfortunately there was no electricity and the radio transmitters were dead, so there was no hope of sending out an S.O.S. or of warning other ships that a derelict was drifting about without lights. It was after midnight when the engineer managed to get an auxiliary motor working and the radio operator was able to send out the first news of the disaster. By then the hulk of the *Petro Queen* had drifted inshore towards Sickle Bay and had leaked most of its enormous cargo into the sea.

As day began to break it was possible to see the terrible disaster that was happening. For three or four kilometres all around the wreck there was a vast slick of oily sludge. Its leading edge seemed to be a living thing. It swayed and probed forward on the surface like an enormous snout. Where the oil was still leaking from deep in the ruptured hold it swung with the movement of the waves, sometimes boiling up in dark underwater storm clouds, sometimes hanging almost motionless like the heads of huge black cauliflowers. But slowly it was spreading up and down the coast, and relentlessly it was moving towards the entrance to Sickle Bay.

Long before sunrise the town was buzzing with activity. Kirsty, Tim and their father were working desperately to help some of their neighbours — stacking furniture outside, hanging out sodden carpets to dry, and temporarily repairing the worst of the damage so that the partly ruined houses could be used again.

Charlie Hilbig was trying to find the main parts of his hotel balcony. One piece was lying like a shipwreck on the verandah of the newsagency and another bit was partly buried out in Captain's paddock. Some people were searching sadly for household possessions, salvaging whatever remnants they could find.

But nobody had suffered as much as Dr Piper and old Mrs Hempel. They had lost everything. Their houses had been standing down on the flats, almost at sea level, and had taken the full force of the tidal wave. Not a floorboard or a gatepost remained. Even the building studs beneath the houses had gone.

Dr Piper stood forlornly where his picket fence had once been, and gazed at the sandswept waste. Kirsty saw him there and went down to join him. He jerked his arm towards the sand.

'The sea is strong,' he said whimsically, 'and very neat.' He paused. 'It must have wanted to read my notes about shells and waterbirds. It's taken them all.'

She tried to cheer him up. 'You'll write them down again — when you've got a nice new house.'

He smiled wryly. 'Don't you think I'm a bit old to be building new houses?'

She shook her head hard. 'Never.'

'Even if I do decide I haven't got anywhere to live while I'm doing it.'

She turned to him earnestly. 'You heard what Dad said. You can stay in the rooms behind the petrol station as long as you like — until your new house is ready. There's even a bathroom.'

He pressed her arm. 'Bless you,' he said simply. 'But I'll have to see. I'll have to think about it.'

They stood silently side by side for a while. 'Have you seen Pinquo?' she asked.

'Not this morning. They've all gone fishing.' He looked at the sand again. 'His burrow is ruined.'

'He'll make another one. He'll dig a burrow while you build a house.'

Dr Piper laughed outright. 'You're a tonic, Kirsty,' he said.

She blushed at his praise and turned her head away. 'Come up and have breakfast,' she said. 'Then Mum'll get your room ready.'

As the day wore on more and more strangers began to arrive in Sickle Bay. Some just came to stand about and gawk and get in the way. Some came to help. They brought news of the damage to other towns up and down the coast, and pointed to the army helicopters clattering overhead, ferrying people to hospital and helping with rescue work. Gangs of workmen arrived to mend telephone cables and electricity lines and water mains. Insurance assessors poked about with notebooks in their hands and stunned expressions on their faces.

'There's nothing like a disaster,' Kirsty's father said sourly, 'to put the town on the map.'

Just after lunch Kirsty and her mother were helping to prepare Dr Piper's rooms behind the petrol station when little Billy Anderson appeared at the door. He was carrying something in an old bag.

'What have you got there?' Kirsty asked.

Billy shuffled and blushed. 'I want to see Dr Piper,' he answered at last.

'Have you got something for him — in the bag?'

'It's a bird,' said Billy, plucking up courage. 'And it can't fly.'

Just then Dr Piper came to the door and Billy hastily repeated his news.

'Well, let's have a look at it.' Dr Piper took the bag, opened it carefully, and slowly lifted out the bird. It was a cormorant. Its feathers were matted and bedraggled, covered in black sludge.

'Good Lord,' said Dr Piper, adjusting his glasses. 'It's covered in oil.'

'Yes,' said Billy. 'Mum said to wash it with soap powder.'

Dr Piper almost dropped the cormorant. 'No,' he shouted, 'no, no, no.' The old man's yell was so fierce that Billy and Kirsty both retreated a step.

'You must *never* use detergents on oiled seabirds. It destroys their insulation and waterproofing. Then they drown or die of cold. Use lard or olive oil if you like — and a clean woollen cloth.'

Billy was so chastened that Kirsty felt sorry for him. 'Where did you find it?' she asked gently.

'On the beach. He couldn't fly.'

Dr Piper was just as worried about the cause as he was about the result. He looked puzzled. 'There must be oil on the water somewhere. Some careless ass has let it escape. Let's hope it's only a small patch.' He turned to Billy. 'Have you got any boxes at home, Billy?'

'I think so.'

'Good. Then keep this fellow nice and snug in a box. I'll come up later on and help you try to clean him up. Don't let him flap about.'

'I won't, Dr Piper.' Billy went off gratefully with his patient.

Kirsty and Dr Piper were about to go back inside when two big trucks came roaring down the main street. One was carrying a motor launch and the other was loaded with drums and hoses. They pulled up near the wreck of the jetty where Bernie Williams was digging out the remains of his fishing boat from the sand. Shortly afterwards a Land Rover with two officials on board stopped at the same spot.

'I wonder what they want?' Kirsty said.

She didn't have long to wait for an answer for just then her father came hurrying around the corner and almost collided with them.

'Did you hear the midday news?' he asked hastily. 'There's been a shipwreck.'

Kirsty's heart seemed to tighten for a second as it always did at a sudden shock. 'Where? What happened?'

'Offshore. A big tanker.'

Dr Piper seemed to catch his breath. 'Oh no.'

At that moment Bernie Williams came running up from the jetty. 'There's been a big oil spill,' he called. 'A tanker close in. Broke her back.'

'Was she loaded?'

'Full up. Crude oil. Almost a hundred-thousand tonnes.'

Dr Piper lowered his eyes as if about to say a prayer. 'God help us,' he said.

'The wave threw her up and she just cracked in halves,' said Bernie. 'The bow sank straight away but the stern's still drifting.'

'How far?' asked Dr Piper fearfully. 'How far out is she?'

'Only a few kilometres. She's drifting in and spewing out more oil as she comes.'

'It'll foul everything up and down the coast in no time,' said Kirsty's father. 'Nothing in the world can stop it.'

'Those fellows are going to spray it — to break it up,' Bernie said. 'But that won't help much.'

'It'll take weeks.'

'It'll be the end of us — of all the fishermen.

It'll kill the fish and foul up the coast for years.'

Dr Piper suddenly seized Bernie by the arm. 'It'll kill the penguins,' he said passionately. 'It'll kill every last one of them within twenty kilometres of Sickle Bay.'

'No,' cried Kirsty. 'No, no!'

'Oil is death to penguins. They can't fly over it like flying birds. To reach the shore they have to go through it. There's no other way.'

They looked despairingly at one another, thinking of a thousand little penguins bunched together on Baker's Knob. Thinking of the warning that had saved the lives of all the people. Thinking of Pinquo.

14

That night the first of the penguins started to come ashore, and by the following day it was clear that the whole penguin colony faced a terrible tragedy.

Dr Piper was beside himself. His white hair trembled with anger and urgency. People later called him the Hornet of Sickle Bay. He set up his headquarters in Mr Kemp's garage and appointed Kirsty and Tim to be his messengers. He forgot all about his own affairs, the rebuilding of his house, even his meals. His only thought was for a thousand little penguins facing a horrible death.

'We need lots of experts to help us,' he said, 'ornithologists, rangers, and wildlife keepers. People who know what they're doing.'

He spent hours on the telephone, making calls to Adelaide, Melbourne, and Sydney. He called up the State Governments, the Departments of Environment, the museums, and the ornithological societies. He called up the Minister of Defence and said he wanted help from the army and the navy. The museums and birdwatching societies promised to send experts and in the end the army promised to send a unit of men to help with supplies and manpower.

When it arrived Dr Piper descended on the army unit like a demon. The poor officer in charge was so stunned that he looked as if he would rather have faced a tank or a rocket-launcher than the little old man with a shock of white hair.

'I want a big tent,' said Dr Piper, 'a marquee and lots of smaller tents.'

The officer gaped.

'And they all have to be up by tonight. Dozens of penguins are coming ashore now and they're all covered in stinking oil.' He paused, his cheeks red with indignation. 'And I want lots of boxes and cartons. And sheets of plastic foam, and newspapers, and plenty of clean woollen cloth.'

'Yes,' said the officer weakly.

'And a lot of codliver oil and lard.'

'Yes.'

'Oh, and a load of pilchards.'

'A load of what?'

'Pilchards.'

'Where am I going to get them from?'

'Anywhere. Fly them from Melbourne by helicopter.'

The officer coughed. 'Yes, doctor. We'll see what we can do.'

Next, Dr Piper gathered together all the schoolchildren and turned them into scouts.

'I want you to go up and down the coast,' he said, 'and find all the sick waterbirds, especially the penguins. Don't chase them or frighten them. They'll be weak enough and frightened enough as it is. Go up to them, slowly and carefully. Take a net or a light blanket to throw over them, and wear some gloves. Then bring them back to me.'

'Yes, Dr Piper,' chirped the search brigade.

Lastly the old man turned to Kirsty and Tim. 'I want you to go with them — one east and one west. You're the overseers. See that they do everything properly. And keep a sharp look-out for banded birds — especially penguins.'

Kirsty looked at him gently. 'Especially Pinquo?' she said.

He smiled sadly. 'Especially Pinquo.'

For the next three weeks Sickle Bay seemed to be the centre of the world. Salvage teams swarmed over it, hurrying to and fro. They were trying to pump the remaining oil from the hulk of the *Petro Queen* into another tanker standing off the coast near by. Day after day anti-pollution teams sprayed the sea and the shore with chemicals to break up the oil. Politicians and visitors and experts of every kind came down to shake their heads and wag their tongues. And in a big marquee down on the flat where Dr Piper's house had once stood a group of men and women and boys and girls worked day and night to save as many of the penguins and waterbirds as they could.

Three or four times a day Kirsty and Tim ranged the shoreline with some of the other searchers. It was a long hard job. Sometimes a new victim had just come ashore and was lying gasping on the sand; at other times some had managed to struggle up the beach to the shelter of the rocks. Each one had to be picked up as gently as possible and carried back to the marquee.

There Dr Piper and his helpers examined them carefully and organised the treatment. Each bird was placed in a box big enough for it to move about in. Plastic foam or woollen cloth — or even thick sheets of newspapers — was spread on the floor, and changed often to help soak up the oil and to prevent infection. Grass and straw were not allowed because Dr Piper said that they could cause lung disease. Then the boxes were placed quietly in the small tents and left there, free of human disturbance.

Most of the worst cases were penguins. Some were already dead. Some were so far gone that they died before anything could be done for them. Some were poisoned by the oil and had to be given drugs by experts. Some had badly matted feathers and had to be smeared with lard or vegetable oil, and then powdered with fuller's earth or cornflour to soak up the excess oil.

Here and there a penguin had been lucky enough to escape with only minor oiling. These Dr Piper powdered lightly and then hosed very gently with warm water or a watering can.

It was all done in stages — slowly, carefully, painstakingly. Before long there were so many penguins in Dr Piper's hospital that the army had to bring in more tents. Kirsty and Tim helped with the feeding. First they had to wrap the bird firmly in a towel to prevent a lot of struggling. Then they dipped a pilchard in water, prised open the bird's beak firmly but kindly, and pushed the fish head-first as far down into the back of the throat as they could. They repeated it again and again, especially with starving birds, until Kirsty wrinkled her nose at the very word 'pilchard' and said she didn't want to see another fish for the rest of her life. She sniffed at herself distastefully. 'I stink,' she said bluntly. 'I stink like a thousand old fish.'

By the end of the second week they had saved almost five hundred penguins. Two hundred had died, and three or four hundred seemed to have disappeared. A good many banded birds had been brought in, including Pinquette and Fisho, and most of them had been saved. But there was still no sign of Pinquo.

'He must have died,' Tim said. 'He probably came ashore further up the coast.'

'He could have swum far away,' Kirsty answered stubbornly. 'He could have swum a thousand kilometres — to Kangaroo Island.'

Tim shook his head. 'Not at this time of the year. He hasn't moulted yet.'

Dr Piper overheard their argument and smiled gently. 'In this business we just have to keep on hoping,' he said to Tim. 'No news is good news.' Kirsty suddenly realised how tired and drawn the old man looked. He had driven himself night and day without rest for three weeks and he was near exhaustion. She felt a great wave of love and pity for him — for his single-minded struggle to save the lives of the little creatures that had saved the town, and that from now on would be linked for ever with its history.

For countries all over the world were hearing about Sickle Bay. The story of the great tidal wave, the saga of the penguins and the way they had saved the people, the wreck of the oil tanker and the people's fight in turn to save the lives of the penguins — all this was being told in newspapers and television programmes around the world.

Visitors poured in to see the town for themselves. Reporters and film cameramen recorded everything in dozens of different ways. Every night various parts of the story could be seen and heard in every sitting-room in the land. And although the local people were sometimes annoyed at the invasion of the town they were secretly proud. More and more of them came down to Dr Piper's marquee and offered to help. Those who were homeless and who were waiting for their houses to be rebuilt said it was a good way of doing something useful; and those whose houses were safe said it was the least they could do to repay the penguins.

Even old Mrs Hempel and Mrs Martin helped. They fetched and carried and cleaned and swept. They made tea and coffee and sandwiches for the other helpers. Charlie Hilbig left his waterlogged hotel for two afternoons each week and went to get a load of fresh pilchards from the cannery down the coast.

Bernie Williams brought in a big tank of fresh water each day on the back of his truck. Mr and Mrs Kemp took it in turns to mind the petrol station so that one of them could go down to the marquee to help. The town had never been so united. The fight for the penguins had joined the people together.

When some of the penguins died during the night Bernie and his son, Sam, and Kirsty and Tim would take them out sadly in the morning and bury them in a deep grave in the sand near their old homes. One day when they had finished doing this Bernie leant on his shovel and looked slowly all about him.

'We ought to fence this off,' he said, 'all the sand patches and the sedge flats and the rocky hollows in the cliffs.'

Kirsty nodded. 'For the penguins?' she said.

'Yes. So that when the sea is clean again they can go back and build their burrows without a lot of human beings trampling all over the place like elephants.'

'Good idea,' said Tim.

'Good idea,' agreed Sam.

They went back to talk to Dr Piper about it, and when he said it would be a wonderful thing for the penguins they discussed it with all the townspeople and the members of the District Council. After that it was just a question of getting the posts and rails and painting them nicely in brown so that it all looked like a little sanctuary or wildlife park. Bernie organised a big working bee. There was not a person in Sickle Bay who didn't come down to help. They finished the job in a single day.

And so the morning dawned when Kirsty was making her usual early scouting trip westward along the coast. Tim was going east. They usually walked for three or four kilometres, just to see whether any penguins had struggled ashore during the night, before they could reach their old homes at Sickle Bay. Later each day a Land Rover drove slowly along the shore for twenty or thirty kilometres to check every part that had been covered by the oil slick. Luckily they were finding very few birds now. Most of them were in Dr Piper's hospital. Or they were dead.

As Kirsty came round a small headland she saw something lying on the beach ahead. It was an untidy black blob, spread-eagled on the sand. Her heart gave a little leap of fear, as it always did when she first glimpsed something like that. Even without a second look she knew what it was — another oil-soaked penguin.

She ran forward quickly, fearful that it was already dead. But as she came up to it the little bird stood up groggily and wavered about for a second as if about to collapse again. To her astonishment it didn't attempt to flee. Instead it turned to face her calmly and even took an unsteady step forward. It was certainly not afraid. There was something about the way it was standing, or trying to stand, that suddenly arrested Kirsty's eye and sent tremors tingling through every nerve in her body — the angle of the head, the droop of the poor blackened flippers. There was a band too, fouled with oil like everything else, but smooth and clearly visible. Kirsty's heart gave a great leap. There was no need for her to look at the number and the printing on the band.

'Pinquo!'

She was down on her knees in the sand, her hands held out towards him.

'Pinquo! Little Pinquo!'

He seemed to be so glad to see her. He took a step forward almost into her outstretched hands, but suddenly toppled sideways and collapsed again.

'Pinquo.'

This time there was fear in her voice and a sudden coldness in her heart. She could see at a glance that he was far gone — cold, shocked, poisoned, starved.

'Oh, Pinquo,' she said over and over again. 'Poor little Pinquo.'

Carefully, very carefully, she picked him up and wrapped him in the small blanket she always carried. Then she turned and ran back towards Sickle Bay as she had never run before.

His body was so light that it seemed to weigh nothing at all. She knew that he was starving. For how long, she wondered, had he been out there in that black and terrible desert looking for food — food that had long since fled or been destroyed. She raced on, holding the little bundle in the blanket gently against her chest — her feet flying, her breath coming in sobs and spasms.

'Pinquo,' she kept saying. 'Oh Pinquo.'

At last she could see the curve of the bay ahead of her, and then the top of the marquee down on the flat. She ran on and staggered in through the canvas opening to the table where Dr Piper was trying to write his records.

'It's Pinquo,' she gasped, collapsing on the chair in front of him. 'I've found Pinquo.'

She placed the blanket bundle on the table.

Dr Piper jumped to his feet. He looked at her intently, asking his question without words. She shook her head sadly, 'He's bad. Very bad.'

Dr Piper took the bundle and unwrapped it gently. He drew in his breath sharply. Then he lifted the little penguin and carried him over to the benches where the sick birds were cleaned and fed.

'Poor little fellow,' he said softly. 'What has mankind done to you?'

Kirsty came over slowly and stood beside him. She could see that behind his glasses he had tears in his eyes.

'Yes,' he said to her sadly. 'He's far gone, far gone.' But then he was himself again — a scientist giving orders and calling on one of the veterinary surgeons for help.

'This one is poisoned,' he said, 'and starved. He'll need a dose of Aureomycin. I want him under intensive care. He's very special.'

He glanced up at Kirsty. Tears were streaming down her cheeks. 'Yes,' she repeated, sobbing. 'He's very very special.'

15

It didn't take long for the news about Pinquo to spread through Sickle Bay. It sent a wave of sadness over the town. All day long people came to Dr Piper's marquee asking quietly for the latest news. They came with hope but went away foreboding.

Kirsty didn't move from Dr Piper's side. Every now and then they went over to the special box that had been set aside in a dark corner of one of the tents, and took off the lid. Sometimes they just checked to see that he was still alive; sometimes they lifted him out very tenderly and gave him another dose of drugs. Whenever she saw his matted feathers and his thin oil-soaked body a big lump rose up in Kirsty's throat and she had to turn her eyes away. They brought in a small heater to keep the box warm and snug.

They tried to feed him but he wouldn't eat. Most of the time he just lay on the floor of his box with his eyes closed. Although they didn't say so, Kirsty and Dr Piper both knew what was happening. Pinquo was dying.

'Why?' said Kirsty, her voice breaking strangely. 'Why must it be Pinquo?'

Dr Piper sighed. 'Sometimes life is hard to understand,' he said simply. 'And so is death.'

'He was so helpless,' she said bitterly. 'He couldn't defend himself. Why couldn't he have been swimming far away when the oil came?'

Dr Piper sighed again. 'Why was there an earthquake in the first place?' he answered quietly. 'Why did the ship happen to be passing Sickle Bay? Why was it a tanker? Why did it break in halves?'

She looked at him miserably. She understood what he was saying but she couldn't accept it. 'It's not fair,' she said angrily.

Tim came in just then and said that it was time for tea, but they shook their heads. Neither of them wanted to eat. The night came on and the other helpers went to bed one by one. Kirsty's mother and father came down and tried to persuade them both to come home but they wouldn't move. And so they stayed on together through the night — the girl and the white-headed old man, and the little creature that was slowly gasping its life away.

From time to time they went over to the box to check it for warmth. Sometimes they lifted the little body but it was limp and listless. Sometimes they shifted the heater or changed the warm cloth in the box. But they were mechanical movements — routine and meaningless.

Just before daybreak when the first faint hint of light began to pale the eastern sky there was a stirring in the camp among the penguins. It was the time when they would normally have begun to leave their burrows to trundle down the beach to the sea. Dr Piper left his chair and went over to Pinquo's box. Kirsty followed him. They both stood there, looking down at the little blackened body. Suddenly his eyes opened and a faint tremor shook his shoulders. It was as if he had heard the call of the sea, the call of his comrades, the deep instinctive call of life itself. He was answering to the great tide that tugged at his spirit, even though his poor bedraggled body was imprisoned for ever. Then his eyes closed again and he lay still.

They tiptoed away and started to prepare for the day.

Kirsty pulled up the tent flaps and Dr Piper stirred the embers under the camp oven.

When they went back a few moments later Pinquo was dead.

It was Bernie Williams who first suggested it. He was talking to Kirsty and Dr Piper later that morning, leaning on his shovel as he always did when he was preparing to bury the little penguins that had died during the night.

'He should be buried in a special place,' Bernie said. 'He deserves it. He deserves a monument.'

'Indeed he does,' answered Dr Piper.

Kirsty's eyes suddenly shone. 'Why don't we?' she said. 'Then people will always remember him. They will never forget his story.'

And so it was agreed. A spot was chosen in the open space beyond the head of the town jetty, and Pinquo was buried sadly and quietly there in a little grave. Bernie marked the place with a simple post.

Before long Dr Piper's struggle to save the penguin colony came to an end. The hulk of the wrecked tanker was emptied and towed away. The oil slick was broken up, and although the shores on either side of Sickle Bay were still fouled with filthy sand and blackened tide marks the sea was habitable again. One by one Dr Piper and his helpers took the penguins back to the shore and set them free. Before long they had rebuilt their burrows and started breeding once more. But the colony was only half the size it had been before. Everyone knew that it would take years for it to recover. And everyone knew that if it hadn't been for Dr Piper and Kirsty and all the people of the town the penguins of Sickle Bay would have been wiped out for ever.

And so the helpers packed up and went away. The army men took down the big marquee and the long row of tents that people had christened 'Penguin Row'. The planks on the jetty were mended and the houses and shops of the town were rebuilt. All except Dr Piper's. He had decided to leave the town and live with his son in Melbourne. Kirsty was sad when he told her.

'Sickle Bay just won't be the same without you,' she said. 'Please stay.'

He laughed gently. 'I'm getting too old,' he

answered. He paused. 'Things change — towns, buildings, people. Especially people.'

She looked at him sceptically. 'You'll never change. Neither will Sickle Bay.'

He shook his head. 'You're wrong. It has changed already. It's not the same town that it was.' She knew what he meant.

'Perhaps it's a better place,' she said.

He nodded. 'I think it is. Better than it was before . . .' He paused, trying to find the right word.

'Before Pinquo,' she said.

He smiled sadly. 'Before Pinquo,' he answered.

On the day before Dr Piper was due to leave Sickle Bay there was a ceremony in the town. A monument had to be unveiled, and he was the person chosen to do it. It was a simple monument — a narrow column of stone about as high as a man, with a life-sized statue of a small creature standing on the top of it. It was a Fairy Penguin with its flippers held out and its head turned slightly at an angle as if its sharp eyes were gazing across the bay to the great ocean that sweeps far away towards Antarctica from the curving coast of Australia.

The monument is there to this day — and so is the little town and the great ocean. It is an ocean where penguins fish and seabirds swoop, where albatrosses roam endlessly over the stormy wastes, and huge tankers hug the coastline, loaded with oil.

A bronze plaque is fixed to the monument, and a patch of green lawn grows all around, with a garden border that is always kept neat and tidy.

And the story of Pinquo lives on there in Sickle Bay for ever.

MORE COLIN THIELE TITLES
from
NEW HOLLAND PUBLISHERS

Storm Boy

The illustrated edition of Colin Thiele's moving story which became a magical film. This is one of the classics of Australian writing for children.

Paintings by renowned artist Robert Ingpen capture the wave-beaten shore and the windswept sandhills of Coorong in South Australia, home of Storm Boy and the pelican Mr Percival.

Storm Boy saves the life of Mr Percival, and in return the pelican helps Storm Boy's father with his fishing and joins in the rescue of a shipwrecked crew. The boy and the pelican prove to be friends to the end.

Magpie Island

The picture book that contains a beautiful story and haunting pictures by Roger Haldane.

> *Magpie shot off like a bolt from a catapult. He whizzed up into the sky above the hill and then swept down in a fierce circle around the she-oaks, his wings hissing through the air like knives.*

Magpie is marooned alone on an island. He is a sad, lonely figure. A castaway. Robinson Crusoe Magpie...

Until young Benny finds him a mate.

Storm Boy and Other Stories

The story of Storm Boy together with five other wonderful Colin Thiele stories feature in this paperback collection.

When Storm Boy goes walking along the beach, or over the sandhills, or in the sanctuary, the birds are not afraid. They know he is a friend.

One of them comes to live with Storm Boy and his father, Hideaway Tom. He is the pelican they call Mr Percival.

This is one of Australia's favourite stories, for everyone knows that birds like Mr Percival never really die.

***Storm Boy* has won many awards. It has been made into a film by the South Australian Film Corporation, and a stage play by the Bell Shakespeare Company.**

Sun on the Stubble

Bruno Gunther lives on a farm in South Australia, where adventures spring up like wheat shoots.

He has to cope with his stern Dad, his Mother and family—and trickiest of all is the new teacher in town, who is too alert for comfort. Then there are the local arguments, that all seem to flare up around complicated bits of machinery, like water pumps and cars.

All they really need is a little help from Bruno to sort everything out...

This is the first of four books that inspired the television series, *Sun on the Stubble*.

Sun on the Stubble Picture Book

This delightful book, especially written by Colin Thiele to accompany *Sun on the Stubble* on television is fully illustrated in colour with still photographs from the series.

There are lots of fascinating people in the little town of Gonunda–Jack Ryan, who drives his car backwards, Hermann Heinz, 'the big tub of lard', Moses Mibus the store-keeper, Uncle Gus, who gets spooked by ghosts, Miss Knightley, the prim schoolteacher.

Then there is Ebenezer Blitz, the half-mad hermit who wants to blow up the general store.

There are lively girls like Laura Kleinig and Louisa Obst, and the three intrepid Gunther sisters.

And of course there is Bruno. After Bruno's adventures, Gonunda can never be the same.

Sun on the Stubble Omnibus

Bruno Gunther lives on a farm in South Australia with his family: his tough and hardy father, strict and loving mother and three lively sisters.

He gets caught up in a series of incidents, including the feud between Jack Ryan and Mr Heinz, who fight about everything, especially cars.

Not to mention the ghosts that roam the roads at night.

Things really get hot when the whole town goes hunting for the wild dog Elijah, and the great Gonunda fire breaks out.

This is the collection of the four books which inspired the television series, *Sun on the Stubble*. They are: *Sun on the Stubble*, *The Valley Between*, *Uncle Gustav's Ghosts*, *The Shadow on the Hills*.